'Idiot,' Jack muttered.

Nicky tipped her head back and peered up at him from the toddler seat in the trolley.

'Not idiot,' she protested indignantly.

'Not you, darling, me. I've forgotten something,' he explained, and with a sigh he shoved the trolley round the corner, nearly crashing into someone.

Someone small, and blonde, and—

'Molly?'

She froze, then turned in slow motion. Her eyes were wide and wary and beautiful, and her lips were working slightly. He had an insane urge to kiss them—

Caroline Anderson has the mind of a butterfly. She's been a nurse, a secretary, a teacher, she once ran her own soft furnishing business, and has now settled on writing. She says, 'I was looking for that elusive something. I finally realised it was variety, and now I have it in abundance. Every book brings new horizons and new friends, and in between books I have learned to be a juggler. My teacher husband John and I have umpteen pets, two horse-mad daughters—Sarah and Hannah—and several acres of Suffolk that nature tries to reclaim every time we turn our backs!' Caroline also writes for the Medical Romance™ series.

Recent titles by the same author:

A FUNNY THING HAPPENED...

KIDS INCLUDED!

BY
CAROLINE ANDERSON

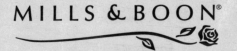

MILLS & BOON®

All the characters in this book have no existence outside the imagination of the author, and have no relation whatsoever to anyone bearing the same name or names. They are not even distantly inspired by any individual known or unknown to the author, and all the incidents are pure invention.

First published in Great Britain 1999
Harlequin Mills & Boon Limited,
Eton House, 18-24 Paradise Road, Richmond, Surrey TW9 1SR

© Caroline Anderson 1999

ISBN 0 263 81750 4

Set in Times Roman 10½ on 12 pt.
02-9908-47855 C1

Printed and bound in Spain
by Litografía Rosés, S.A., Barcelona

PROLOGUE

'ABRACADABRA!'

The coins vanished from one hand and reappeared magically in the other, to the amazement of the children sitting cross-legged in front of her, watching her every move with wide-eyed anticipation…

At least, that was the theory.

In practice, the coins fell out of her hand, rolled across the floor and wobbled to a halt just in front of the first row of straight-faced and sceptical little monsters. They laughed and scrabbled for the coins, the magic hopelessly blown away, and Molly sighed.

Darn Sandy and her wretched wrist—

She dredged up a smile.

'Ah. Well, how about this trick?' she suggested, and waved Sandy's wand again. Her fingers disappeared up her sleeve, hunted around for a moment, then came out with a stream of brightly coloured handkerchiefs.

In theory.

She looked at the single yellow square in disgust. Obviously her knots left something to be desired…

She rootled around in her sleeve again for the rest of the colourful string, and the children tittered and giggled and nudged each other. In the back corner a man sat, watching her steadily as she poked about for the elusive end. He was the host—Jack something. Hallam? Haddon? He would have made a good poker player, she thought crossly as she rummaged. Totally po-faced, he was the

5

man who, if she pulled this off, would pay her for her services.

Hah. The only thing she was going to pull off was the lining of the jacket, and as for being paid for this fiasco—!

Molly's face flamed, but she persevered, and they began to laugh louder. 'I know they're up here somewhere,' she muttered, and the laugh grew to a crescendo. The man was still watching her intently. His mouth twitched, and she could have hit him, or strangled him with the brightly coloured silk squares—if she ever found them.

She could feel them tugging over her shoulder, so she stuck her hand down the back of her neck and pulled, and, yes! Out they came!

The children roared their approval, laughing and clapping, and to her astonishment Molly realised that they were enjoying it. They thought—bless their little cotton socks—that she *meant* to camp it up! And the man with the money was laughing, too!

Thank God for small mercies, she thought wildly, and plunged on with the act.

Everything went wrong. She didn't mean it to, but she didn't really have to try. Sandy made it look so easy— just wait till she caught up with her!

'Help me out—my wrist is so bad I can't possibly do the tricks—'

Well, Sandy wasn't the only one who couldn't possibly do the tricks, but at least the children seemed to be on her side now. The rings steadfastly refused to come apart, the disappearing balls under the cups kept appearing again, the card trick ended with cards scattering like confetti—and through it all they laughed like little drains.

Only one more trick to go, and that was sure to get them all going. She set the top hat on the table, flicked the catch and put her hand in. Yes, she could feel it; she had its little silky ears—

'Ouch!'

She leapt back, the hat and table went flying, and the star of the grand finale headed off across the floor of the hotel function room at a flat-out hop.

Molly, sucking her bitten finger, swore silently and violently for a moment, then, hitching up Sandy's baggy magician's pants, she squeezed and wriggled her way through the crowd after Flopsy.

The children were all scampering about chasing the rabbit, and Molly saw it make a run for it towards the corner with That Man. If she headed it off—

She leapt over a table, scooted across the room and dropped to her knees, skidding the last two yards into the corner. Arms outstretched for the rabbit, she dived after it as it headed for the safety of his chair.

Almost—

She stretched out her hands, toppled forwards and grabbed, and ended up with her hands fastened firmly round the rabbit—and her shoulder propped against his thigh. His firm thigh. Oh, help.

Victorious, and not a little flustered, she sat back on her heels and smiled up at him witlessly. Her hair was on end, her cheeks were flushed and she was laughing. So was he—except she had the distinct and uncomfortable feeling he was laughing at her.

The rabbit wriggled, and she dived forwards again. She wasn't letting go of that damn rabbit for anyone. Just another inch—

She lost her balance, what little was left of it, and slowly, like an action replay on the television, she toppled over and ended up face-down in his jeans-clad and very masculine lap. Heat scalded her cheeks, and she wriggled backwards, digging her chin into his thigh to lift her head.

'Ouch!'

Firm, strong hands cupped her shoulders and lifted her away before she could do any lasting damage. His eyes were sparkling, his lips twitching with amusement and something else—something very male and distracting that took the last of her breath away.

'I know the advert said the show had a wonderful climax,' he murmured, laughter threading his voice, 'but never in my wildest dreams…!'

CHAPTER ONE

'BUT I *want* a lolly!'

'Later, darling.'

She scanned the shop anxiously. He couldn't be here! Of all the places, and of all the people to run into all these miles away, it would have to be *him*!

If it was him, of course. It might not be—if she was lucky. If she wasn't—and just recently her luck had been running somewhat thin—she could only imagine what it would do to their holiday!

Heat scalded her cheeks. The last time they'd met—the *only* time they'd met, in fact—had been a disaster. She could still vividly remember the embarrassment, the chaos, the pandemonium—

'Mummy, *please*!'

'Pretty please, with a cherry on top, an' loads of juicy cream?'

'You did promise us.'

She closed her eyes in defeat. Cassie was right; she had promised them— 'All right, then, just this once. Go and choose, then come and find me. I'll carry on.'

And hopefully Haddon and his handful of hooligans wouldn't see her...

It *was* her. He was sure—certain of it. She'd made enough of an impact, after all, he thought with grim humour. He hurried round the corner, pushing the trolley round the aisles of the little supermarket, searching for another glimpse.

She was so damn small, of course—five foot in thick socks, and as skinny as her rabbit.

Well, perhaps not skinny, he amended, remembering the soft curves pressed against him as she'd chased the rabbit under his chair and cornered it finally, with her breasts forced against his shins and her chin resting in his lap in a very tantalising and inviting way.

She'd been flushed to the roots of that lovely natural blonde hair, her dazzling blue-green eyes wide with laughter and apology and something else—something he hadn't had time to investigate but which had played havoc with his sleep pattern for weeks.

He hadn't been able to contact her. The real magician— the proper one that he'd booked for the kids' party—had been most evasive when he'd rung. He'd been offered a refund, but that wasn't what he had wanted.

What he'd wanted, however, had been too difficult to explain—if he'd even known himself. So he'd been forced to give up.

And now here she was, more than a year later, in the same adventure holiday village as them.

With someone?

He felt a stab of disappointment, and squashed it with a silent chuckle. 'Idiot,' he muttered, and Nicky tipped her head back and peered up at him from the toddler seat in the trolley.

'Not idiot,' she protested indignantly.

'Not you, darling, me. I've forgotten something,' he explained feebly, and with a sigh he shoved the trolley round the corner, nearly crashing into someone.

Someone small, and blonde, and—

'Molly?'

She froze, then turned in slow motion. Her eyes were

wide and wary and beautiful, and her lips were working slightly. He had an insane urge to kiss them—

'Do I know you?' she asked with commendable cool.

Jack stifled a chuckle of admiration. He'd been a cop for too many years to mistake someone at this range—especially this someone. He smiled at her over Nicky's head. 'Jack Haddon—you did a party for my son Tom a year ago.'

Her eyes flared with panic, but she kept her cool. 'There must be some mistake,' she began, but then Seb and Amy and Tom came charging round the corner and slithered to a halt, staring at her in delight.

'It's Molly the Magician!' Tom yelled, and the colour in her cheeks slid up into her hair and darkened to a fetching crimson.

'Hi, kids,' she said weakly, and he met her eye and waited. She swallowed and smiled feebly. 'Um—yes, I think I remember now.'

'You brought a rabbit, and it ran away under the seats,' Amy reminded her.

'And we all chased it, and you caught it under Jack's chair, but it got frightened and wee'd on you,' Tom added.

She gave a breathless little giggle and bit her lips to trap the laugh. 'So it did. Well, nice to see you again.' She edged away, her eyes flying up to meet Jack's and then flying away again. 'Have a nice holiday.'

'You, too.' Then he added, because he was suddenly very curious, 'Are you here all week?'

'Um—yes.'

His heart, unaccountably, soared, and his mouth quirked into a smile of its own accord. 'Good. I'll see you round.'

Molly returned the open, friendly smile a little distractedly, and made her escape. She couldn't believe he didn't hate her. It had been the most dreadful party.

She gave a little moan of anguish at the memory, just as her kids came running up. 'We've got orange lollies,' her son said. Her daughter gave her a keen look.

'Are you all right? You made a funny noise, and you're a very strange colour.'

She pasted on a smile. 'I'm fine. Come on, guys, we've got to find out where you need to be in the morning, and we have to go back and unpack, and then maybe we'll have time for a swim—'

She was gabbling, running off at the mouth a mile a minute, but it was all his fault. He just turned her inside out with that knowing, sexy smile and those laughing eyes—

'Damn.'

'Mummy!'

She hadn't realised she'd said it out loud. She threw an apologetic glance at her son. He was looking mildly scandalised and a little fascinated, because she simply didn't swear—at least, not aloud, and certainly not in front of them. 'Sorry, Philip. Right, let's go and pay for this lot and we can go back to our cabin.'

Unloading the shopping half an hour later was a chastening experience. Bread, but no butter or marge. Peanut butter—they all *hated* peanut butter; she hadn't bought it since David left—oven chips, a small pepperoni pizza, a pint of skimmed milk, not semi-skimmed as usual—the list of oddities and inconsistencies rambled on. Blue cheese, a tin of tuna, no salad or teabags—the man had distracted her so badly she couldn't think.

'So, what's for supper?' Philip asked curiously, eyeing the collection with distaste.

'Um—I'm not sure. I've forgotten one or two things.'

'We could eat out—they've got a pizza place in the square,' Cassie was kind enough to point out.

'Yeah, can we?' Philip asked, his eyes wide and hopeful. They never ate out.

Molly, who cooked for a living, thought it sounded a very good idea all of a sudden. 'Fine. I'll put this lot in the fridge and we'll go and swim, sort out where we all have to be and then have supper.'

The pool was wonderful. There was a wave machine, a flume, wild water rapids, a swirly river thing that swept you round an island, and, best of all, a hot whirlpool tub. The kids were strong swimmers, and sensible, so after they'd explored the pool complex together, she sent them off with strict instructions to keep an eye on each other and wallowed in the hot tub, watching out for them as they climbed the steps to the top of the flume.

'Mind if I join you?'

Her heart jolted wildly, and she looked up to be treated to acres of muscular, hairy thigh and lean washboard abs that made her want to moan out loud.

'Feel free,' she croaked, shuffling up a little, and he squeezed in beside her. They were hardly alone, there were two other couples in the big round tub, and Molly was intensely grateful for them. Safety in numbers, she thought a little hysterically, and then wondered what on earth she was worried about. He thought she was a complete twit. Who wouldn't, after the way she'd performed?

He settled in beside her with a big sigh, and she was enormously aware of him just inches away. His foot brushed hers, and she jumped as if she'd been bitten and shuffled a little further away.

He smiled knowingly. 'Sorry,' he murmured, but she knew he wasn't. Damn.

They sat in silence, cosseted by the bubbles, while she tried not to think about his lean and very masculine body, so close she could reach out and touch it—and then the other couples climbed out and left them.

Molly scooted round a bit, not quite opposite him but not so close, either. 'Where are the children?' she asked to fill the silence and to quell the riot in her mind.

'Seb's keeping an eye on them. They all swim like fish, even Nicky, but he's got her in the paddling pool and the others are going on the flume. I thought I'd take five, and Seb knows where I am.' He propped his head back and closed his eyes with a sigh. 'Are you here on your own?' he asked lazily.

'No—I've got the children with me.'

His eyes flew open. 'Children?'

'Yes, children. You know, those little bits of DNA that grow up to persecute us?'

He chuckled. 'Them,' he said with a smile, and studied her searchingly. 'I didn't realise you had children. You look too young. Are they in the crèche?'

She laughed a little wildly. 'You have to be kidding. They'd skin me alive before they let me put them in there.'

He glanced around. 'So are they with your husband?'

'Um—no. I—ah—we're here alone. They're swimming.'

His eyes widened. 'They can't be old enough! Not unless you started at ten.'

Her laugh was getting a little hysterical. 'You are *too* kind. I think you also need your eyes checked. I have grey hairs, and bald bits where I've yanked the grey out, and wrinkles you could hide inside!'

'And I've parked my Zimmer just round that rock.'

She laughed again, softly this time. 'I'm thirty-one—and you're a million miles from needing a walking frame.'

He grinned. 'At the moment, but I have a hideous feeling that's all going to change. I'm doing a mountain-bike ride with Nicky on the back tomorrow morning that will probably kill me, even though it's supposed to be gentle, and then in the afternoon for my sins I'm abseiling with Seb while the others do canoeing and finger painting variously.'

'Let me guess—the baby's finger painting.'

'Yup. I hate to think what state she'll come back in.'

'She'll be fine—send her in something old and tatty.' Molly shifted a little so she could see him better. 'So, where's your wife while all this is going on?'

He met her eyes with a clear, level gaze. 'I don't have a wife. Where's your husband?'

And that was direct! She filed the information about his wife and answered him frankly. 'Australia—dodging the maintenance payments.'

'Ah. Hence the magic act.'

'No, not at all. That was to help out a friend.'

'You were good.'

'I was awful.'

'I thought you were very funny.'

She gave a strangled laugh. 'It was meant to be slick and fast and magical—not a take-off of Tommy Cooper.'

He tipped his head and grinned. 'I could see you in a fez. I don't suppose you want to do a repeat performance—?'

She laughed and shook her head. 'Oh, no. It was definitely a one-off. Never again.'

He stretched, and she tucked her feet up just to be on the safe side.

'So, what do you do, then?'

'I'm a nursery nurse—except I'm not. I used to run a crèche but I needed to be around in the school holidays after they grew up a bit, so I did a cookery course and now I've got a catering business. I make sandwiches and deliver them to various outlets every day, and I do the odd bit of catering for dinner parties and wedding buffets.' She tipped her head a little and studied him. 'So what do you do? Apart from keeping up with the children?'

He grinned, a lop-sided tilt of his mouth that creased his eyes and softened the angular planes of his face and made her heart hiccup. 'I write crime novels—detective stories about people perpetrating convoluted and bizarre crimes on unsuspecting members of the public.'

She chuckled. 'Like me, you mean?'

'Absolutely. My current heroine is a little like you. She's small and feisty—she's a victim, but she escapes the final thrust and lives to tell the tale.'

'I'm so glad,' she said with a smile, and wondered if his heroine *was* like her, or if he was just being flattering. 'Where do you get your ideas?'

His face closed a little. 'I was a cop,' he said lightly, but his eyes were suddenly shielded.

I was a cop. Just that, but it told her so much—and asked a million more questions. Like, had it been the end of his marriage—?

'Did she walk out?'

He blinked. 'She?'

'Your wife.'

His mouth hardened, and she flushed and sat up in a flurry of bubbles and arms and legs. 'Sorry, that was intrusive.'

To her surprise he answered. 'Yes, it was—and yes, she did. She found it all too much.'

'And left you with the kids.'

He looked down into the water. 'Not exactly. Look, I have to go. I'll see you around.' He sat forward. 'Where's your cabin?'

'Area B—by the lake.' What did *not exactly* mean?

'So's ours. What number?'

'B15.'

'We're B19—I'll look out for you. Perhaps we can get together—it would make a change to talk to another adult. Talking to a strand of mutant DNA gets a little tedious at times.'

His mouth quirked, taking the edge off his words, and he stood up. Water streamed off his body, running in rivulets down his arms and legs and that fascinating chest with the little vee of hair between the nipples—

'Jack?'

She looked behind him at the boy standing there, a little girl in his arms. They were nothing like him, the boy tow-haired and wiry, the girl blonde and baby-plump, reaching out chubby arms to her father. The oldest and the youngest of his brood, she remembered.

He took the baby in his arms and kissed her, then grinned at the boy.

'Thanks, Seb. Going on the flume?'

'The rapids. Amy and Tom are after an ice-cream.'

His voice cracked and he coloured, flicking Molly an embarrassed glance.

Puberty, she thought, was such a painful thing. Jack looked at her. 'Why don't you round up your children and join us at the pool bar?'

She shook her head and stood up, conscious of her figure in the snug black one-piece that left none of her curves or dimples to the imagination. 'Sorry, no time. We have to check where we're going tomorrow, and then apparently I'm treating them to pizza. Thanks, anyway.'

He nodded, his eyes sweeping her body, and she forced herself to stand straight and tall under his scrutiny. Well, straight, at least. It was difficult to stand tall when you were barely five foot.

'We'll see you round.'

She nodded, and watched as they went off together. Seb was quite a different shape from his father, she thought, watching them. Wiry and not so tall, but probably going to head on up and overtake him in time.

Like Philip. He was all arms and legs at the moment. Perhaps he'd grow into his height before he went up any more. She hoped so, because just now he looked like a stick insect.

Cassie, though, was tiny and dainty and just like her mother.

She wondered again what he'd meant by *not exactly* when she'd asked if his wife had gone off and left him with the kids. What a strange response. And they called him Jack.

Her curiosity piqued, she picked up her towel, hugged it round her shoulders and picked her way carefully round to the queues for the flume and rapids.

A boy cannoned into her and grinned, and she recognised him as Tom, Jack's youngest boy, with a girl— Amy, was it?—in tow. Her own weren't far behind, and she had to go on the rapids with them twice before she was allowed to drag them off to the activity checking point.

Philip was doing water sports all the next day, and Cassie was riding in the morning and canoeing in the afternoon.

So she'd see Jack and his brood again tomorrow anyway.

Odd, that little flicker of hope the thought generated.

*   *   *

Jack wondered what Molly was doing. Not the 'gentle' mountain-bike trek he was on, anyway.

Sensible woman.

His legs killed, his chest heaved, his body was streaming with sweat—and he'd thought he was fit!

Hah!

Nicky's hot, sticky little hands on his back didn't help, but it was curiously comforting to have her close like this. He wondered how the others were getting on—and what Molly was doing.

Watercolours? A pampering massage?

He groaned silently at the thought of her body stretched out naked, smeared with green gloop, with some unknown masseur kneading and squeezing the muscles.

Lucky b—

'Jack?'

'Hi, Nicky. You OK, sweetheart?' He turned his head and smiled at her, and her little sunny face beamed back at him.

'Need a wee,' she announced cheerfully.

Oh, hell. It was the second time, and each time he'd had to struggle to catch up.

The joys of parenthood. Oh, well, perhaps sweating up the hill after the others would settle his libido down and quieten his raging hormones...

Molly stood on the edge of the building, her feet braced against the side, her body hanging out into free space, and wondered what on earth she was doing.

Abseiling?

For *fun*?

'Just pass the rope through that hand and pay it out bit by bit—that's it. That's fine. You're doing really well.'

She was? Sweat was breaking out all over her face, and

the soles of her feet were crawling with nerves. The ground seemed a zillion miles away.

Still, it could have been worse. If she'd been on the afternoon course, she would have had Jack watching her. It would have put her off so badly she probably would have dropped like a stone.

She might anyway, just thinking about him! She forced herself to concentrate before she killed herself and left her children without a mother...

'Hi, Tom. Good day?'

'Brilliant! I learned to roll over in the canoe and come up again, and—ugh, what's happened to Nicky?'

Jack grimaced. 'Finger painting.'

'Looks more like face painting.'

'Mmm. Where's Amy?'

'Oh, she's got a friend. There she is—her name's Cassie.'

Jack looked, and his heart slammed against his ribs. Molly was coming down the beach towards the girls, smiling that lovely bubbly smile that used every muscle in her face, crinkling her eyes and tilting her nose and widening that kissable, soft mouth—

Hell.

'That's Molly the Magician,' Tom said, looking longingly at her. 'She was really cool. She must be Cassie's mum.'

'Must be,' Jack murmured, looking at Molly every bit as longingly. She reached Cassie and hugged her briefly, and he wondered what it would feel like to be the recipient of that hug. The child was the spitting image of her mother, but without the sex appeal. No doubt she'd get it in spades once she was older, and her mother would have her hands full fending off would-be suitors.

His gaze switched to Amy, a darker blonde, more mousy, with pale skin and clear blue eyes, just like her mother. Jack felt a pang of sorrow and hugged little Nicky closer. 'Shall we go and get Amy?'

And, coincidentally, bump into Molly again. She didn't notice them approaching, so his greedy eyes absorbed every detail of her. She looked good enough to eat in shorts and a skimpy top that did terminal things to his blood pressure. Those legs—

'Hello, Molly,' he said softly.

She looked up, her eyes wide, and those delectable lips tilted. 'Hi, there,' she said with that open, ingenuous smile that did him in. 'Picking up the kids?'

'Yes.' His voice was gruff and sounded as if he hadn't used it for a month. He cleared his throat. 'Had a good day?' *How was the massage?* Blast. Quell that thought.

'Fine—bit scary. I was abseiling this morning. I must have been mad. How about you?'

Jack found himself grinning like a Cheshire cat—a tom cat, to be exact. 'The mountain-bike trek was all up-hill, all the way round.'

'That's not possible,' she said with a laugh.

'Oh, it is. Believe me. They hire someone to tilt the earth—they must.'

She chuckled again. 'And your abseiling?'

'A piece of cake by comparison. I was so busy worrying about Seb I hardly noticed my own descents.'

She looked around. 'Where is he?'

'Gone back to the cabin. I said we'd meet him there.'

She nodded and looked around. 'Philip! Come on, darling.'

Philip came, apparently very reluctantly, and somehow they ended up on their bikes all heading back in the same direction.

It seemed as natural as breathing to offer them all a drink as they wobbled back into Area B, and after a second's hesitation that Amy and Cassie's pleading overwhelmed, Molly gave him a wary smile and accepted.

His heart thumped again, and for a ridiculous second he felt as if he'd asked her out on a date.

Absurd...

The cabin wasn't really big enough for eight of them, but he threw open the patio doors and they spilled out onto the short, scrubby grass beside the lake. Ducks came waddling up expectantly, and within moments Nicky was there asking for bread for them.

He absent-mindedly handed her a slice and searched the fridge. Not enough orange for all of them; not enough of anything. He needed to go shopping again.

He diluted the juice, used small glasses and watched Molly as discreetly as he could.

He was watching her. Probably looking for imminent signs of madness. She couldn't believe that he'd really liked the magic show, and there was no way it was her legs he was studying, so it must be the lunatic tendencies he was waiting for.

'So, what's on tomorrow?' she asked.

'Ah—tomorrow. Monday? Let's see—Seb's bungee-jumping and doing some commando thing, Amy's doing the theatre workshop all day and Tom's skateboarding and trail-biking, I think. How about you?'

'The same, I think. I know Philip's trail-biking in the afternoon, and Cassie's certainly doing the theatre workshop. She'll enjoy that, being with Amy. They seem to get on very well.'

His eyes tracked to the children. 'They do. I'm glad. I was wondering how it would work, but finding a holiday that suited all five of us was a nightmare. Usually at least some of us are bored some of the time, but I don't think we're going to have time to be bored this week.'

She chuckled. 'No. I think we're going to be pooped instead. I feel tired already! What about the little one?'

'Nicky?' Again his eyes tracked to her, as they often did, his internal radar keeping tabs on the active youngster, she thought. 'I think Nicky and I are in the farmyard tomorrow morning, and then in the afternoon she's in the kindergarten and I'm kart racing.'

'So am I!' she exclaimed, and then could have bitten her tongue out. Did she have to sound so enthusiastic? He'd think she was following him round! Oh, Lord, her and her big mouth—

'That's great,' he said, and he sounded sincere and— interested? No. He was just glad to have company. It was a bit daunting joining new groups every session, having to work with total strangers. It was easier if there was someone there that you'd seen before.

That was all he meant—surely?

'What about the morning?' he asked.

'I was going to have a lazy couple of hours with a book,' she confessed.

'You could always join us in the farmyard,' he suggested.

Was that interest in his eyes? Possibly. Oh, lawks. Nobody had looked at her like that for so long she wasn't even sure!

'Thanks—I'll think about it,' she said, vowing to do no such thing. No, she'd lie in the bath, read a book, pamper herself with body lotion and a thorough facial treatment, and lie in the sun.

'I tell you what, if you're coming, let me know before eight-thirty.'

'I will,' she agreed, knowing she wouldn't do any such thing.

No way was she walking round a farmyard with a man with lazy, sexy eyes and four children. Oh, no!

CHAPTER TWO

'MOLLY?'

She jerked up into a sitting position, her lids flying open, and met Jack's laughing eyes with an inward groan.

'Hi,' she mumbled through stiff lips. She tried to smile, and felt the skin shatter all over her face. Her hands flew up and covered the hideous mask, and with a moan of anguish she flopped back against the sun lounger and glared at him. 'I thought you were at the farmyard?' she wailed, cracking furiously.

He grinned, quite unabashed at having caught her in such disarray. Damn.

'Seems I wasn't needed there.'

You're not needed here, she nearly retorted, scrambling to her feet and clutching the sides of her dressing gown together. The only good thing about it was that he couldn't see the flaming colour in her cheeks under the crumbling face pack.

'Give me a minute,' she muttered, and felt a chunk of the vile green mud flake and fall off. She fled for the sanctuary of her bathroom, trailed by a masculine chuckle that did nothing for her temper—or her equilibrium.

Ruthlessly she crumbled the face pack and scrubbed it off with warm water, slapped on some moisturiser that made her go all shiny as well as pink, and dragged on her shorts and T-shirt. Hmm. She looked about sixteen— which, come to think of it, had to be an improvement on thirty-one.

She shoved her feet into sandals, wriggling into them

as she walked, and found him sprawled on her sun lounger, face tipped up to the sun, eyes shut, utterly at ease.

'Coffee?' she snapped, and he opened one eye and squinted at her in the sunlight.

'If you're sure it's no trouble.'

'It's no trouble,' she said ungraciously, and flounced back into the cabin. Fancy catching her like that! She'd looked a total fright! He might have warned her he was coming! She banged around in the little open-plan kitchen area, smacking mugs down on the worktop, popping the seal on the instant coffee and tapping her foot while the kettle slowly came to the boil.

'You're mad with me.'

Her head jerked up and she glared at him over the kettle. 'Why should I be mad with you?'

He smiled understandingly. 'Because I caught you looking like a refugee from a frog pond?'

She stifled the smile. 'You have such a way with words.'

He laughed, propping his arms on the half-wall that surrounded the kitchen area and leaning over towards her with that engaging grin of his. 'Am I supposed to say you looked ravishing?'

'And add lying to your sins?'

'Maybe it's not a lie.'

'And maybe you're a frog. That would explain a lot.'

He smiled. 'You could always kiss me and see if I turn into a prince.'

Her heart unaccountably thumped. 'In your dreams,' she shot back, refusing to smile.

'Grouch.'

'You'd better believe it. I'm not my sunny best when I'm caught like that.'

He straightened up, his mouth twitching. 'I don't suppose there's any point in telling you you'd look wonderful covered in mud from head to foot?'

She arched a brow. 'Hardly. I'd only think you had a kink about women mud-wrestlers—either that or you really are a frog.'

His eyes sparkled with humour and he let the smile out, drawing her attention to the firm fullness of his lips and the hard angle of his beautifully-sculpted jaw. Perhaps she ought to kiss him and find out—?

'Penny for them.'

She laughed then. 'No way. Black or white?'

'Black—strong, no sugar.'

How had she known that? She handed him the mug over the little wall, and scooping up her own she went out into the little sun-trap patio at the back of the cabin. Like his, it looked out over the lake and was open to anyone who chose to walk past it—the last place she should have sat with her face pack on.

She'd thought she was safe, though, because there hadn't seemed to be anyone about. It was just her luck that he'd come looking for her and found her like that! She sat on one of the chairs at the picnic table, tucking her legs up under the chair and chasing a little pine-needle round the table top.

He sat down on her right, looking out over the lake, his legs stretched out under the table and crossed at the ankle. She hitched hers a little tighter under her, out of reach. No way was she playing footsie with him with the cabin just behind them and not a child in sight to protect her from his abundant charms!

'Gorgeous morning.' He stretched his arms over his head, locking his fingers behind his neck and yawning hugely. His T-shirt drew taut over the muscles on his chest, and she had to drag her eyes away before she disgraced herself.

She stared at the lake, counting ducks until her heartrate was back under control.

'So, how come you weren't needed?' she asked to fill the silence—and when she could trust herself to speak.

'They had enough helpers, and Nicky seemed quite happy. She'd got to know one of them yesterday doing finger painting, apparently.'

'So you thought you'd come and persecute me?' she asked with a smile to take away the offence. Actually, she was quite pleased he had, despite the face pack. He was fun, and it seemed like years since she'd had fun—even if she didn't intend to play footsie.

'Something like that,' he replied with a smile, and his eyes were warm and kind and crinkly at the corners, as if he did it often. It made her go all gooey inside—which was ridiculous, considering he couldn't possibly be really interested in her. He was just passing the time. Idle flirting. Most men did it, like breathing, without even noticing.

He drank his coffee, then peered into the bottom of the mug and set it down with transparent and very obvious regret.

'More?' she offered automatically.

The smile was lazy and sexy and satisfied. 'I will if you will.'

For a moment she wondered what he was talking about, but then collected her scattered wits. 'I'm fine—I usually only have one.'

He sat up, the smile fading, searching her face. 'I'll go if you want to get back to your vegetative state.'

She laughed and stood up, scooping up his mug. 'No, I've vegged enough. Black again?'

'Please.'

She made the coffee and took it out, setting it down in front of him. 'There was some research done a while ago that linked strong black coffee with sterility, but I guess if you've got four children that rather blows their research away,' she said with a grin.

Something changed in his eyes, and he gave a short, humourless grunt of laughter. 'We may never know,' he said quietly. 'They're not my kids.'

'Not—?' Molly swallowed and dragged in a lungful of air. There she went again, she thought, jumping in with both feet.

'Not yours?' she finished, still on autopilot, wondering all sorts of things. Like, if not his, then whose? Was he their uncle? Godfather? Guardian? Friend? Stepfather, maybe. They called him Jack. And where were their real parents? Was his ex-wife their mother? And where had the parents been a year ago at that dreadful party—?

'Their parents are dead,' he told her, answering at least one of the questions.

A wave of regret washed over her, drowning the frenzied thoughts for the moment. 'I'm sorry,' she murmured automatically. 'How awful for them. How? What happened?'

He sighed. 'Nick was my partner—we worked together,' he told her, his voice expressionless. 'He was shot working under cover. His wife was just pregnant with Nicky at the time, and he didn't know. Then while she was pregnant she found out she had cancer.'

'Oh, no.' Molly put her hand over her mouth, stemming the questions, letting Jack talk. After a moment he went on.

'They couldn't treat it because of the baby. She died when Nicky was five months old.'

'And you took the children on,' she added softly, aching for them all.

'Yes. I'm Tom's godfather anyway. I married Jan just before Nicky was born.'

Whatever she'd expected, it hadn't been that. 'You didn't waste any time,' she said without thinking, and his face hardened.

'There wasn't a lot of time to waste,' he said harshly, and scraped back his chair. 'I'd better go and pick Nicky up. Thanks for the coffee.'

And he went, leaving the full mug slopping gently on the plastic table. She mopped it up mechanically, throwing the coffee down the sink, and wondered how she'd grown so tactless in her old age. Fancy accusing him of marrying the children's mother in undue haste, without knowing anything except the barest outline—and she only knew that because she'd blundered onto the subject by talking about sterility!

'What a fool,' she muttered, and wondered if he'd ever speak to her again. Probably not. He'd probably ignore her, and she'd deserve it. Damn.

And then she forgot her own problems and remembered the children, Seb and Amy and Tom, who must have grieved bitterly for their parents, and little Nicky, who had never seen her father and wouldn't remember her mother, and the ache that had been growing for the last few minutes welled up and spilled over.

What had it been like for Jack, losing his friend and then his—well, wife, really, she supposed. Had he loved her for years? And the children—how had they coped?

She sniffed and scrubbed away the tears. Poor little things. Fancy growing up without a mother. Who would cuddle them when they were hurt and frightened, and tell them—especially Amy and Nicky—all the things girls needed to know and boys needed to understand?

Jack, of course, being mother and father to them.

And what kind of a man was Jack to take them all on? He must be a complete fool, or an angel. Either that or he *had* loved their mother—perhaps was Nicky's father, even—and he was doing it out of guilt.

Whatever, he was doing it, and the vast majority of men would have run a mile before they'd take on such a responsibility.

Her estimation of him went up another notch, and she wondered yet again if she'd damaged their tentative friendship beyond repair. She hoped not, because if ever a man needed help it was this one, and, for some crazy reason she just couldn't fathom, she wanted to be the person to give it…

Jack waited by the entrance to the go-kart rink, looking out for Molly. She'd said she was karting this afternoon, and he owed her an apology for storming off like that. He'd just had so much of it from Jan's mother, and initially from the children, too. He hadn't wanted to deal with it again, but even so he should have expected her reaction and stayed to explain the reasons to her.

Instead he'd flounced off like a toddler with a tantrum, and probably left her upset and confused.

Damn.

There she was, dressed in jeans and trainers and a T-shirt, walking tentatively towards him. He went to meet her.

'I'm sorry—'

'I'm sorry—'

He gave a rueful laugh, and she smiled, cautious and

uneasy. 'I never should have said it. Why you married her is none of my business.'

'I should have explained—I know all the things going through your head; I've heard them all. Let's just say for now it was for the kids. I'll tell you more later—if you'll listen?'

The strain left her face. 'Of course I'll listen,' she said, and he felt as if a weight had been taken off his chest.

'Good. Right, let's see if frogs can drive karts.'

'Meaning you, or me?'

He grinned. 'Either. Both.'

'Speak for yourself.'

'Ribbet-ribbet.'

He saw the laughter bubble up inside her, transforming her worried expression. 'Idiot,' she said, and he grinned again, absurdly pleased with himself for making her smile and bringing the light back into those gorgeous blue-green eyes.

He was disgustingly good at karting. She struggled to control the feisty little machine, but Jack didn't seem to have any such problem. He whipped past her time and time again, his focus absolute, his concentration mind-boggling.

When they stopped, he unravelled himself from the little rollerskate of a kart and stretched, grinning from ear to ear. 'That was brilliant. I haven't done that for ages.'

'I haven't done it ever,' she said drily, 'and it shows.'

He chuckled. 'You did fine.'

'You didn't even see me. You were going too fast to notice.'

'Oh, I noticed.' His mouth quirked and he searched her eyes. 'We need to fetch the kids. I'd better go; I have to be in three places at once.'

'Why don't I get the boys? Then you can pick up the girls—the theatre workshop's quite near the kindergarten, and the trail-bikes are right over on the other side. It would make sense.'

He nodded thoughtfully. 'You sure? That would be great.'

He did have the most gorgeous eyes, she mused. 'Absolutely sure. I'll meet you back at the cabins in a bit.'

He waved her off at the bike park, and she headed across the site, following the wiggly paths amongst the cabins until she reached the trail-bikes.

The boys were just coming out, looking grubby and cheerful, and she waved to them.

'Where's Jack?' Tom asked, peering round.

'Picking up the girls. You're both coming back with me and we're meeting up at the cabin. Have a good time?'

'Brilliant!' Philip said. He could hardly keep his feet on the ground he was so high, and Tom was the same. They went ahead, chattering all the way back to the cabin while she struggled to keep them in sight, and threw their bikes down and rushed round the back to find the others. She propped the bikes up, locked them and followed more slowly.

Jack was there with the girls, sprawled behind his cabin on a sun lounger, Nicky draped over his chest fast asleep while the boys blasted Seb with a loud and chaotic resumé of their trail-biking exploits.

She sat on the grass beside Jack and tipped her head towards Nicky. 'She looks bushed,' she said quietly.

'Busy day. She's only two and a half; it's all a bit much. I might take tomorrow morning off and do something quiet with her.'

Molly grinned. 'You're just looking for a way out—too much activity for your old bones.'

He gave her a wry grin. 'You'd better believe it. I'm supposed to be doing a paintball game with Seb tomorrow—all that crashing about in the woods getting scratched to bits and dolloped with paint—I can hardly wait.'

'You'll love it.'

He snorted, then looked down, his fingers playing idly with the baby's blonde locks. 'Maybe, but she's tired. I don't think she can cope with another busy day.'

'I'll have her if you like,' she offered, before her brain took over.

'You're mad.'

She smiled, covering up her regret at yet another impulse. 'Probably. I like little children. We can feed the ducks and read a book and make biscuits, and she can have a nap if she needs it.'

He looked thoughtful—because he didn't trust her? Because she'd sounded forced and over-jolly? She must be nuts. If anyone needed a day off she did—and then she looked at the dark shadows under Jack's eyes, and the lines of fatigue in his cheeks, and her soft heart melted all over again.

'I am a trained nursery nurse,' she reminded him gently, 'and I've brought up two children alone for the past five years. I can cope.'

He pursed his lips, then nodded, swallowing. 'If you really don't mind. I can't be everywhere at once and I feel I ought to spend some time with Seb doing man stuff, you know?'

She smiled softly. 'Yes, I know. I have a friend I bribe occasionally to do "man stuff" with Philip. You go and have fun with Seb. It's just too easy to forget how important these little things are.'

He nodded. 'Tell me about it. I spend my life juggling—and most of the time I drop all the balls.'

'I'm sure you don't. The kids all look well and happy.'

'I try.' He looked down at Nicky again, then at Molly. 'I'd offer you a cup of tea, but she looks too comfy to move.'

'I'll get you one.'

'Bless you.' The smile crinkled his eyes, just a little, an almost imperceptible softening of his features. It made him devastatingly attractive—at least to Molly. She stood up hastily, brushed off her jeans and went into the kitchen. It was the same layout as hers, so finding things was easy, which was just as well because that tiny smile had utterly scrambled her brains…

They met just after nine, when the five younger children were safely tucked up in bed and Seb was slouched in front of the television. Jack appeared at the patio doors at the back of her cabin, and together they strolled down to the lakeside.

It was a beautiful evening, the sun's last rays dying over the water and touching the trees with gold. Ducks and geese glided silently over the surface of the lake, rippling the still water and scattering the sunlight.

It was peaceful and beautiful, and they sat down together on the edge of the water and just absorbed the stillness for a while.

It was amazingly quiet. There was the occasional sound of laughter, a child crying in the distance, and here and there the odd call of a bird or scuttle of a vole.

Beside her Molly could feel Jack thinking—could almost hear the cogs turn. Maybe he didn't know where to start. Maybe he needed help.

'Tell me about Jan,' she prompted gently.

Jack's sigh was soft and full of regret. 'Jan? She was stocky and feisty and loud, and Nick adored her. It was mutual—she thought the sun rose and set on him. They fell in love at sixteen, married at twenty, had Seb at twenty-three. His parents hated her—she was a little off the wall for their taste, and they never really trusted her. When Jan found out she was dying, they said they'd have the children. She couldn't bear the idea, but she had no choice. Her own parents were dead; she couldn't see another way.'

'Until you suggested one.'

He looked down at his hands. 'Nick had asked me, years ago, if I'd have their kids if anything happened to them. I was married then, they'd only had only Seb and Amy, and I said yes. Nick had it put in his will, but Jan thought everything had changed so much I wouldn't have them—not all four. As I saw it, they needed me even more. I suggested we got married, and I adopted the children. It was what Nick would have wanted, and it gave Jan the security she needed to die in peace.'

'And the children?'

'Amy and Tom were OK, and Nicky was too tiny to know what was going on.'

'And Seb?'

He sighed. 'Seb thought it was awful. He couldn't understand why they couldn't go to his grandparents and he could look after them all there. He was twelve, too young to cope, too old to be told what to do without questioning it. And he didn't like the thought of me touching his mother.'

'And did you?'

He shot her a searching look. 'Hardly. She was my best friend's wife, a real one-man woman. She was dying of cancer. Of course I didn't touch her. I didn't want to. That wasn't what it was about.'

Molly felt relief for a moment, but there was another question she and her foolish mouth just had to ask. 'Did you love her?'

'Yes. As a friend, as a wonderful mother to my godson, as an incredible and beautiful human being—yes, I loved her. As a woman—no. Not in that way. I never once looked at her and envied Nick anything but his relationship with her. That I would have given my eye teeth for, but Jan herself? No. She wasn't my type. Does that answer your question?'

Her smile was wry. 'I think so. And Nick's parents—did they take it lying down?'

Jack laughed humourlessly. 'You are joking. They went up the wall. They wanted the children, said they could cope. Now, they won't even have them all at once for the weekend because they're too much!'

'And are they too much for you?' she probed softly.

He chuckled and threw a little stone into the lake, watching the ripples spread. 'Only most of the time. Sometimes—usually when they're asleep—I can almost cope.'

She could hear the love and despair in his voice, and wanted to hug him. Instead she slid her hand over the mossy turf and threaded her fingers through his, squeezing silently.

'I think you're amazing taking them on,' she said quietly. 'Most men would have handed them over to their grandparents with a heartfelt sigh and legged it.'

'Nick would have had mine,' he said, and something in his voice said it all.

She wanted to cry for him. 'He must have been a good friend.'

'He was the best.'

His voice sounded raw and hurt, and his fingers tightened on hers. She returned the pressure, offering wordless comfort, and after a moment the pressure eased and he sighed. 'It's crazy, I still miss him.'

'I'm sure you do.' Her mind rambled on, dealing with the nitty-gritty, imagining life in his household—imagining a week-day morning in term-time, with everybody's homework lost on the kitchen table, three lunches to get, Nicky to wash and dress, buses to catch—hideous. 'It's a good job you were already writing,' she added. 'You couldn't have looked after the children if you'd been at work.'

'I was at work. I gave up. Luckily my writing was just taking off and I was able to pull out of the force and just about manage to live on my earnings.'

She shifted a little, turning towards him. 'But the children must be provided for—you don't have to pay everything for them, do you?'

He shook his head. 'No. There is a fund I can call on, but I'm trying not to. They'll need it when they're older. It's their inheritance.'

He slipped his fingers out of hers and stood up, holding his hand out again to draw her to her feet. 'Walk?' he suggested, and she cast an anxious glance back at her cabin, where her children were sleeping.

The sun had set now, and the village was settling into darkness. She didn't like leaving them, but she sensed Jack needed this time out from his brood. She nodded. 'All right—but just a little way—not out of sight.'

'OK.'

They strolled along the water's edge, not talking, not quite touching, sharing a companionable silence. Every now and then one of them scuffed a little stone, and it would roll into the water and send a ripple out across the surface.

'It's so peaceful,' Jack murmured.

'Mmm.' She looked across the lake to the village centre, a hub of activity even this late at night, and at the edge, beside the water, she could see a restaurant. Lights from it twinkled in the lake, and she could see the faint flickering glow of candles on the tables.

'It looks very romantic,' she said, and could have kicked herself for the wistful tone in her voice.

She needn't have worried. Jack was looking at it just as wistfully. 'It would be nice to have a meal there without the kids,' he murmured. 'How about it? Shall we share a babysitter, order the kids pizza and go and paint the town red?'

The thought was wonderful. 'Sounds good,' she replied, gazing across the water. 'Do you suppose they do babysitters?'

'I think so. We can ask tomorrow. What's on your agenda?'

She laughed. 'I have no idea. Babysitting Nicky while you're doing man stuff with Seb, otherwise I don't know. The kids are sailing again, I think, and I might have a totally lazy day or maybe go swimming.'

'Sounds good. The paintball game is first thing—if you're sure about Nicky?'

'If she'll come to me.'

'She will. She's used to it, bless her—and then, if we can, we'll go out tomorrow night and try and remember how we misspent our youth!'

Molly laughed. 'Speak for yourself. My youth was exemplary.'

'High time you started living a little, then,' he murmured, and his voice slithered down her spine like melted chocolate, leaving a shiver in its wake.

And Molly suddenly had the feeling that a quiet dinner *à deux* in the candlelit restaurant by the lake might be a very foolish move indeed...

CHAPTER THREE

As Jack had promised, Nicky was quite happy to be left with her. A placid, cheerful child, she was perfectly content up to her elbows in flour and biscuit dough.

They baked, and, because Nicky wanted to play with the leftovers, Molly found leaves and helped her press them into the dough to make patterns of veins. They used coins and keys and all sorts of things to make patterns, and Nicky thought it was wonderful.

They had to make up more dough, and ended up with more on the child than on the table. Then they cooked the messy bits of dough for the ducks, cleaned up a bit and sat down to eat some of the proper biscuits which they'd made first.

The ducks were delighted with the bits and pieces, and Molly's soft heart warmed watching Nicky laughing as the ducks pecked up the crumbs. She was so sweet, so spontaneously cheerful, so delicious. Her mother would have loved her dearly.

Oh, blast.

She sniffed and blinked, swallowing the tears, and, taking the trusting little hand in hers, they went for a wander by the lake. She'd brought some of the left-over biscuits with her, and gave them to Nicky to throw out into the water for a family of ducklings that hovered just out of range, curious but a little wary.

They got braver, until finally one came and pecked a biscuit right out of Nicky's fingers.

Her shriek of delight sent it scurrying back to Mum,

and Nicky turned her laughing face up to Molly. 'It pecked my finger!' she said, quite undaunted, and Molly laughed and hugged her.

'Come on, let's go and see what else we can find.'

They locked up and set off on foot for the toddlers' adventure playground that was located near their cabins. Nicky had fun, scrambling over the logs and climbing little ladders, crawling through tunnels, sliding down miniature slides.

She was wary of the chain and log bridge, a swinging, jangling, somewhat unstable structure that had Molly crossing her fingers and hovering at the side, but she did it in the end, and after a couple of tries she was running across it, laughing as it bounced and swayed under her weight.

After she'd sat in a tyre swing and Molly had pushed her till her arms ached, they strolled back to the cabin through the woodland, watching a squirrel for a few minutes as it skittered around on the pine-needle floor before disappearing up a tree.

'Hungry,' Nicky announced as they let themselves in. 'Nicky have lunch.'

'OK.' Molly opened the fridge and looked. Thank goodness she'd been shopping again and taken her brain with her. She shuffled the contents. Peanut butter. Better not, she didn't know if the child was allergic to it, and, if she'd never had peanuts, Molly didn't want to be the one to find out!

They had a quick-fix tuna and pasta bake in the end, and a nice crunchy salad that she was pleased to see Nicky ate quite happily. All through the messy eating of her yoghurt the little girl rubbed her eyes, and so when they were finished Molly took her to the bathroom, then snuggled down with her on the sofa in front of the television.

There was a children's channel with a lovely little cartoon, and after a few minutes Molly felt Nicky go heavy beside her. A tiny snore escaped her, and with a smile she settled the little one down on a cushion, made herself another cup of tea and wondered if they would be going out that night. Jack was going to see if he could make a reservation and arrange a babysitter, and she wouldn't know until he got back.

And if he'd been able to set it all up, there was another problem—what was she going to wear?

A quick glance through the wardrobe proved what she'd already known—she had nothing with her suitable for knocking the socks off a man with lazy, sexy eyes and a mouth she was just aching to kiss!

Jack was sore. He'd been scratched and bitten in the undergrowth, shot at from all directions and generally tortured by the whole experience. Running at a crouch, zigzagging through the bracken and crawling flat on his stomach were things from his past, things he'd done long ago and thought he'd left behind.

And he'd enjoyed it.

Perverse! Seb had enjoyed it, too, and seemed particularly proud that neither of them had been 'killed' by the 'enemy'. Jack was glad they'd both got through it without getting hurt or lost. He wondered how the younger kids were, and if they'd been all right left for the day. They'd had a packed lunch, and all of them were doing watersports for the whole day, so they were together at least.

And Nicky, he thought, was with Molly and would be fine.

Funny how he just knew that. He'd had to trust people with her over the past couple of years, just to get anything done in his life, but he'd hated doing it. Now, leaving her with Molly, he felt completely at ease.

Because she was a woman, not a child. A real woman, with children and responsibilities and common sense.

And the sexiest legs he'd seen in ages, and soft curves, and a wide, smiley mouth that nearly did him in.

He groaned, and Seb shot him a curious glance. 'You all right?'

'I'll live—just a few aches. I'm not as young as you,' he flannelled, and cuffed Seb gently round the head. 'You all right, sport?'

'Yeah—that was cool. We trashed them,' he added victoriously.

'Mmm. I think we ought to get back—make sure Molly's all right. I expect by now Nicky's driving her up the wall.'

Seb chuckled. 'Probably. We could always buy pizza or something tonight so we don't have to cook to make up for it.'

'Ah—I need to check something on the way home. I was going to take Molly out for a meal as a thank-you and get a babysitter for all you kids together, with a few pizzas and some popcorn or something.'

Seb looked utterly unimpressed. 'A babysitter,' he said flatly.

'For her children, really,' Jack added, hastily soothing his ruffled feathers. 'We thought it would be more fun for Amy and Cassie and Tom and Philip if they were together, and if it's in our cabin then Nicky can just go to bed, and I felt it was too much to ask you to cope with all of them alone.'

Seb screwed up his face thoughtfully. 'Do I *have* to be there?' he asked.

Jack recognised the tone of voice. There was something

else coming—some hidden agenda that was probably going to have emerged later. 'Where else did you want to go?' he asked carefully.

Seb scuffed a stone with his toe and shrugged nonchalantly. 'There's a disco in the village square—fourteens to eighteens. I thought I might give it a look.'

'What time?'

'Eight till eleven.'

Jack nodded slowly. 'Well, I don't see why not. You're sensible. Can you make your own way there and back? We'll be at the Lakeside Restaurant—if they can find a babysitter for us, that is. You can always come and find us.'

Only please don't, he added mentally as they climbed into the minibus that took them back to the village centre. Let me have this one evening alone with her—just a little time out, a glimpse of how it used to be, when I had the time and the energy and the opportunity for socialising.

Nothing else, though. Not with Molly. It wouldn't be fair.

Well, maybe a kiss. Just one.

Or two.

Nothing more…

'It's all arranged,' Jack told her, lounging in the doorway as he picked Nicky up. 'Babysitter's coming at seven-thirty and so's the pizza, Seb's going out at eight to the disco in the village square and our table's booked for eight-thirty, so if we leave once the pizza arrives, we can have a drink first.'

Molly smiled a little stiffly. 'Great. Thanks,' she murmured. Her heart was thumping, her head ached and all she could think was that she didn't have a decent dress to wear and she wanted to look her best—

'What is it?'

He looked worried, studying her searchingly with those eyes that could see the slightest nuance of her emotions. Policeman's eyes that missed nothing. She shrugged and tried to laugh. 'I'm being silly. I haven't really got anything to wear.'

His face cleared and he smiled, reaching out to graze his knuckles gently over her cheek. 'You'll be fine in anything. Have you got a skirt?'

She nodded. 'I've got a dress, but it's a sundress really. I suppose if I wear a cardigan over it to cover up the bare bits…'

'Seems a shame,' he murmured, and she was reminded of his remark about it being time she learned to enjoy life.

Oh, lawks.

'Maybe if I wear enough make-up and jewellery it won't look odd,' she mused.

'I'm sure you'll be fine. It doesn't matter, anyway. So long as you aren't downright scruffy they won't worry.'

But I will, she thought, because I haven't had a date in what feels like a hundred years, and for some reason this really does matter to me. She looked up into his grey eyes, their expression gentle and reassuring, and all of a sudden she didn't care because she knew he didn't.

Perhaps he didn't see it as a date.

Somehow, that didn't comfort her as it should have. She thought about it all through bathing the children and getting them ready for bed, through putting on her sundress—a plain white dress with scoopy neck and no sleeves that was a little short for elegance—through fiddling with the bead necklace that dressed it up a little, through the last critical glance in the mirror that probably wasn't necessary, and then she told herself to stop fretting and trundled them along to Jack's at seven twenty-five.

He just wanted a companion for the night, just someone to take out and talk sense to, an adult instead of a child— just someone to keep him company while he slipped the leash for a while.

If she could only bear that in mind, do the same thing, just enjoy it for what it was—if she could only do that without wondering what it would be like if he kissed her—then they might get through the evening without her making a complete fool of herself.

The kids banged on the door and let themselves in, instantly absorbed into the hubbub and chaos. The baby-sitter was already there, the pizza arrived right behind her, and Jack put the box down on the coffee table in the lounge area, gave Seb and the babysitter last-minute in-structions about what time Seb was to come in, where to contact them and so forth, and hustled her out of the door with a warm, firm hand on the small of her back.

The door closed behind them, he paused for breath and shot her a crooked grin. 'Shall we go?'

She smiled back, the grin cheering her. 'Sure. Is the dress really OK?'

His eyes swept over her slowly, then came back to her face, something disturbing in their expression. 'It's lovely,' he said gruffly. 'You look gorgeous.' He hesi-tated, then cleared his throat. 'Right, let's go.'

They walked in silence, slightly apart, only unlike last night something crackled between them, some indefinable tension that interfered with her breathing and made her heart beat slow and hard against her ribs.

'So, how was the paintball game?' she asked to break the tension.

He laughed. 'Tiring. Wake me up if I topple over into my soup,' he said drily. 'I'm too old for that sort of thing.'

She chuckled. 'Anyone with any common sense—' she

said, and left the sentence hanging. 'Still, did Seb enjoy the man stuff?'

'I think so.' His mouth quirked. 'We won, anyway, so honour was satisfied, thank God. At least we won't have to do it again. My ribs have got a scrape on them from a branch that was intent on revenge, and my knees are bruised from crawling over stones, but apart from that I'm just peachy.'

'Poor old man,' she murmured teasingly. 'I'll have to look after you, I can see.'

'Absolutely. I need Molly-coddling. Don't you think that's appropriate?'

She shot him a look. 'Don't hold your breath,' she said. 'I only Molly-coddle those really in need.'

'I'm in need!' he protested. 'I ache from end to end.'

'More fool you. You should have known better than to go crawling around in the woods at your age.'

He gave a wry chuckle. 'I can see I'm going to get a lot of sympathy from you over this. I shall have to re-member not to commiserate when you tell me Nicky was awful.'

'Nicky was wonderful. We had lots of fun. She's a real sweetheart—in fact, they all are. They're a credit to you, Jack.'

He coloured slightly, cleared his throat and looked down at his feet, scuffing the stones like an awkward ad-olescent. 'I do my best. Sometimes it isn't enough.'

She laughed sympathetically. 'Tell me about it! You do everything you can, and then they turn round and say you don't understand them, or you don't love them, or there's no point talking to you because you just don't listen.'

'Sounds like Seb.'

'Has it been difficult with him?'

'He's been the hardest to get through to. At first, particularly, he challenged my authority over everything. He would say, ''You're not my father, you can't tell me what to do,'' and there was no way to deal with it except to say that his father had trusted me with his care and I was doing what I thought he would have wanted me to do.'

'And did that work?'

He laughed ruefully. 'Not always. He'd tell me I hadn't known Nick as well as I thought and he used to let him do whatever the current gripe was about, which I knew to be a load of rubbish. Still, we got through it. It's better now. I think I'm earning his respect at last, but it's been uphill all the way.'

He ushered her through the door of the restaurant, and they were immediately wrapped around by the tranquil, romantic atmosphere. Soft music filtered from the walls, strategically placed plants gave tables a cosy intimacy, and there wasn't a child in sight. Bliss, Molly thought with a smile.

Despite the peaceful atmosphere it was busy, but she could see a door open at the other side of the restaurant that seemed to lead to an outside seating area draped with a living screen of vines and clematis.

He must have read her mind. 'We've got half an hour. Shall we go outside with our drinks while it's still warm enough?' he suggested, and she nodded.

'Please. It looks lovely.'

Jack ordered their drinks and led her out onto the terrace, right down at the water's edge. The vines hung over a pergola, draping around them and giving the evening sun a soft greenish light. It was a little like being underwater, she thought.

There was a table at the edge, and Jack nodded his head at it. 'OK here?'

'Lovely—at the moment.'

'Tell me if you get cold or eaten alive, and we'll go inside.'

She smiled, touched by his solicitousness. He was such a kind man—he would have to be, to take on four children. She wondered how he managed to keep sane.

A waiter brought them menus to study, and Molly looked at the bewildering array of expensive dishes and decided she'd been crazy to agree to come out with him. Her half of the bill was going to be stupendous!

'What's the matter?'

'Just the choice,' she lied.

Jack put his menu down and sprawled back in the chair. 'Have whatever takes your fancy—in fact, do you want to split the lobster? I haven't had lobster for years.'

Nor had she, and she was sick of counting the cost of everything. She dropped the menu on the table and grinned at him. 'Sounds good.'

Blow the cost. She'd done terminal damage to their budget with this holiday, anyway, but they'd all been so tired and crabby and in need of a change. She just hoped she'd still think it was worth it a few months down the line when she was still struggling to pay the bills!

'So, tell me all about yourself.'

She looked up at him, startled by the directness of his gently voiced command. 'Me?' she murmured. 'I'm deadly dull.'

He snorted softly. 'I think not.'

'I am. I get up in the morning, make sandwiches, get the kids off to school, deliver the sandwiches, shop for the next day, feed the kids, fight about homework and fall into bed.'

'And what do you dream about, Molly?' he asked quietly. 'When you fall into your lonely bed at night, what fantasies torment you?'

She flushed and looked away. 'I don't have fantasies. I'm too tired.'

'Always?'

'Always,' she lied.

He gave a weary laugh. 'I know the feeling. Oh, well, it was worth a try.' He paused, one long, blunt finger chasing the slice of lemon that floated in his gin and tonic, then he looked up and speared her with those searching eyes. 'Why did your husband leave?' he asked softly.

'David?' She looked out over the lake, watching the ducks making golden wakes in the sunset. 'Responsibility is a tedious thing when you're God's gift. Staying at home with us, doing chores, going shopping, watching television in the evening instead of going out—it was all too pedestrian.'

'So what happened?' Jack prompted when she stopped talking.

'He started playing away.' Good heavens, was that her voice, so calm and rational? She'd been far from calm and rational at the time, and when he'd announced that he was leaving her and going to Australia to get away from them all, she'd been almost relieved. At least she wouldn't have to deal with the lies and subversive remarks and continual criticism—

'Bastard,' Jack said, very quietly under his breath, but loud enough for her to hear.

Molly shrugged her shoulders. 'He was just young and felt trapped. We should never have got married. We were only nineteen at the time.'

'Nick and Jan were only twenty,' he said harshly.

'Some people are ready then.'

'And others are never ready,' he added with a lack of expression that made her realise he was talking about his ex-wife. She waited, but he added nothing, staring blankly out over the water.

Then he drained his glass and stood up. 'Another?' he asked, holding out his hand for her glass, but she shook her head.

'I'm all right for now.'

He disappeared into the bar, as much, she felt, to give himself time to put the past back where it belonged as to get another drink. He reappeared in moments, a bottle of mineral water dangling from his fingers, and set the fresh glass down on the table. She felt tension seep out of her. She'd thought he might be about to drown his sorrows or drink his way through the evening.

It seemed she'd judged him harshly.

'Can we do something?' she said.

He arched an enquiring brow.

'Can we leave the past alone tonight? Forget it exists? Just be us—talk about the things we like, and the places we want to go, and the things we want to do?'

His mouth curved gently, and he tilted his glass of innocent water at her in a silent toast. 'Good idea,' he murmured. 'You go first. What's your favourite colour?'

'Green,' she said promptly. 'Dark, foresty green. What's yours?'

'Blue—soft, smoky blue, like faded denim. Or maybe charcoal-grey. What's your favourite food?'

'Lobster, I think. I can't remember.'

He chuckled. 'Mine's definitely chocolate mousse—rich, black, home-made, with a hefty slug of brandy in the bottom and a huge dollop of cream on top.'

Her mouth watered. 'Oh, yum,' she said. 'Can I change my mind?'

He laughed again. 'Ladies' prerogative, isn't it? What about films?'

'*Brief Encounter*,' she said. 'Or *Pretty Woman*.'

'Romance,' he said, settling back. 'I knew it.'

'What about you?' she prompted.

He looked uncomfortable. 'Well—*Where Eagles Dare*, maybe, or probably *Casablanca*, if I'm honest.'

She laughed. 'Romance again. Book?'

'Oh, that's harder. There are so many all-time greats. I like the modern crime writers, but I also like John le Carré and Agatha Christie and the classics, like *Jane Eyre* and *Pride and Prejudice*.'

'More romance,' she teased.

'All part of life's rich tapestry,' he said easily. 'Love and sex and revenge and murder and deviousness and deceit and forgiveness—they're all there.'

'You forgot faithfulness and kindness and duty and responsibility and cherishing and nurturing.'

His smile faded. 'I didn't forget them,' he corrected. 'I just didn't mention them. I don't forget them. Maybe I didn't mention them because they're so fundamental.'

'Not to everyone,' she said quietly.

'Hey.' He leant forwards and brushed her cheek with his knuckles. 'We were leaving the past where it belongs, remember?'

She looked up into his face, into the searching eyes filled with kindness and compassion, and she wanted to hurl herself into his arms.

Instead she gave him a shaky smile and sat back. 'Good idea,' she answered, and looked away. All that kindness could be addictive—that warmth and compassion and strength and gentleness—

'Your table's ready for you, sir,' a waiter murmured, appearing discreetly at their sides.

'Molly?'

She looked up at him, gathered her bag and stood, following the waiter through into the dining area. He seated them at a cosy, intimate table, surrounded by lush plants and lit by a small group of candles in the centre.

It was elegant, private and altogether too romantic for her common sense to deal with. She felt herself being lulled, lured by the moment and the man, and she hardly noticed the food.

The lobster was wonderful, but couldn't hold a candle to Jack's warm and lively conversation. The chocolate mousse was wicked and decadent and no kind of a match for his eyes, and by the time they'd sipped their way through a bottle of smooth, mellow wine and finished off with Irish coffee, she felt as if she was floating on cotton wool.

He paid the bill, ignoring her feeble protests. 'When I take a woman out for dinner I don't expect her to pay for it,' he said firmly, and that was the end of that.

He ushered her out into the cool, dark night, and when she shivered he draped his arm around her shoulders and drew her against his side. The walk back to the cabin was only short, but every step was torture, the hard nudge of his hip against hers, the heavy warmth of his arm, the heady scent of soap and something more personal, more intimate, more—Jack.

He paused at the path to her cabin. It was dimly lit, the curtains closed, the light on in the kitchen to make it look occupied. 'It's only ten,' he murmured. 'It seems a shame to waste the rest of the evening.'

She met his eyes in the soft glow from the street lamps dotted along the path. She would be foolish to ask him in. She knew what would happen, what fate had in store for them.

'Coffee?' she suggested, and her voice was a thready sigh.

'Maybe.'

She closed her eyes and let him lead her up the garden path. How appropriate.

The key wouldn't fit the lock, and Jack had to do it for her. He didn't have a great deal more success, but finally they were in, and the door closed softly behind him.

'Molly?' he murmured.

Panic swamped her. She couldn't do this, couldn't make love with a man she scarcely knew—

'Molly, stop it.'

'Stop what?' she said, clutching the kettle like a lifeline.

'I'm not going to do anything. I just wanted a little more time with you, to round off the evening. Don't be frightened.'

She gave a brittle little laugh. 'I'm not frightened, Jack,' she assured him. She plugged the kettle in, lifted down two mugs and set them on the worktop. 'Sit down,' she said, 'make yourself at home.'

He did, propping himself up in the corner of one of the two settees, one ankle propped on the other knee, his arms spread out across the back and side of the settee, watching her. He hadn't put the lights on over there, so the only light was the overspill from the kitchen spot lamps, and she couldn't read the expression in his eyes.

He looked very male and inviting and a little predatory, and she spilt the coffee granules on the worktop because he made her hands tremble with something she hadn't felt for years.

Anticipation? Hunger?

Wanton hussy, she scolded herself, but she knew she wasn't. She was just lonely and empty, and so was he, and that was terribly, terribly dangerous. She was right to be frightened of the force of this thing between them.

She wiped the worktop and took the coffee over, hers

weak and white, his black and strong. Yin and yang, day and night, light and shade.

He sat up a little and sipped his coffee, and she perched on the other settee and clutched her coffee mug like a crucifix to ward off evil.

'That was a wonderful meal,' she said into the throbbing silence. 'Thank you.'

'My pleasure. Thank you for looking after Nicky.'

She gave a strained little laugh. 'You could have taken her to kindergarten and saved a fortune.'

'But it wouldn't have been nearly such fun.'

'No.' Her hand shook a little and the coffee slopped against her skin, making her wince. 'Damn,' she murmured, and stood up to get a cloth just as Jack rose, too. She put her hand out to steady herself and it came to rest on his ribs, making him wince.

'Sorry!' she cried. 'Is that where the branch got you?'

He gave a wry grin. 'Spot on,' he murmured. 'Don't worry.'

'Let me see,' she ordered, and pulled his shirt out of his trousers, hitching it up.

The warm, smooth skin was scuffed, a wide scrape the length of her hand slashing across the bottom of his ribcage. It looked angry and sore, and without thinking she dropped her head and laid her lips against it.

He tensed and, shocked, she drew away. 'Sorry,' she muttered. 'I don't know what I was thinking about. Just— habit, to kiss things better. I do it all the time with the kids.'

She looked up into his eyes, laughing and yet stormy with something that she'd brought to life. 'I ache all over,' he said softly. 'Kiss me better, Molly.'

She couldn't help herself. With a strangled sigh she went into his arms, careful to avoid the damaged ribs, and his mouth, that beautiful, chiselled, laughing mouth came down on hers with the touch of an angel's wing, and she was lost.

He held her gently, his lips grazing hers, dragging over the soft skin of her throat, testing the pulse that beat like a wild bird in the hollow under her chin. His tongue caressed her, making a shiver run through her body, and a tiny moan of need rose from some long-forgotten place in her heart.

'Molly,' he groaned, his breath hot against her throat, and then his mouth found hers again, demanding this time, his tongue probing, seeking. She gave him what he asked for, then demanded it back, her hands sliding up to cup his head, steadying it, her fingers threading through the soft, silky strands of his hair.

He tasted of coffee and after-dinner mints, and his mouth was skilful and clever and wicked, making her want things she'd thought she'd put behind her. She arched against him and his hands moved, leaving her back, sliding round and up to cup the aching fullness of her breasts, and then with a ragged groan he broke the kiss.

'I want you,' he said unsteadily, his breath hot against her mouth, his chest heaving with the wild passion that was surging through him. 'Molly, stop me,' he pleaded. 'This is crazy.'

'No,' she whispered, pulling his head down to hers again, her lips cold without his. 'Please, Jack—love me.'

He groaned and moved away again, releasing her, stepping back, holding her at arm's length. 'Molly, no. We can't.'

'Please—'

'Molly, you'll get pregnant.'

That stopped her, as nothing else could have done.

'Oh, Lord,' she said shakily, and sank down onto the settee, her legs useless.

He sat beside her, one arm round her, his free hand grasping both of hers in a death grip. 'It's OK,' he said gruffly. 'Just give yourself a minute.'

She felt tears clogging her lashes, and squeezed her eyes shut. 'I'm sorry,' she whispered. 'Lord, whatever must you think of me?'

His arm tightened, drawing her against his chest. 'Molly, stop it. I want you just as much. There's nothing wrong with that. We just mustn't let it run away with us.'

'But I want to!' she wailed softly, turning her face into his shoulder.

His voice was gentle. 'I know,' he sighed. 'Believe me, I know.'

He released her, standing up and going to the kitchen, turning on the kettle again. 'I think we need coffee.'

'It's still here.'

'It's cold. I'll make some more.'

She sat numbly, still stunned by the force of the need he'd released in her. She'd never felt like this in her life— never!

'Here.'

He set the fresh coffee down in front of her, retreated to the safety of the other settee and watched her over his mug as he sipped the scalding brew and waited for her to come to her senses.

'I'm sorry,' she said eventually, picking up her mug. 'I'm an idiot.'

'No. You're lonely, and so am I. You're also very, very beautiful—'

'Oh, Jack, don't be silly.'

'You are. I don't care if your husband never told you that; it doesn't stop it being true.'

She met his eyes, and saw the truth in them—at least the truth as he believed it—and that made her feel beautiful, for the first time in her life. 'Thank you,' she whispered, and the tears welled up and splashed down her cheeks.

'Oh, God, Molly, don't, or you'll do me in,' he groaned. 'It's difficult enough as it is.'

'I'm sorry. Nobody's—oh, hell.'

She sniffed, scrubbing her nose on the back of her hand, and then she picked up her coffee and made herself drink it.

Then she put the empty mug down and looked at her watch. 'It's nearly eleven.'

'I know. We ought to go.'

She nodded and stood up, rounding up keys and bag and her cardigan against the chilly night air. At the door, she paused. 'Jack—thanks for tonight. For all of it.'

He drew her into his arms.

'Don't thank me. You can't know what you've given me tonight. Just let me hold you for a moment.'

She did, resting her head on his chest, listening to the rhythmic beat of his heart and the soft sigh of his breathing. It was so good to be in someone's arms—someone she could trust, someone she could rely on—even if only for now, for this moment.

He dropped a kiss on the top of her head, hugged her again and released her gently. 'Let's go and see how much chaos they've caused,' he said, and opened the door.

CHAPTER FOUR

THE rest of the week passed in a rush of activity and organised chaos. The children were busy, dashing from one venue to another for their various sports, and her contact with Jack was often no more than a brief encounter at the moment of pick-up and drop-off.

He didn't ask her to have Nicky again, and she didn't offer. She didn't want it to look as if she were angling for another meal with him, although she would have loved it. Instead they kept it all very low-key, with no time to be alone, no time to test out the strength of their resolve in the face of the passion they'd awakened.

Which was just as well, Molly thought, as she didn't think her resolve had the strength of a wet paper hankie.

They'd packed everything into her car on the last morning, and she'd waved to Jack as he walked up and down their path doing the same thing. Then Cassie turned to her.

'Can we go and say goodbye?' she asked. 'Please, Mummy, we won't see them again for *ages*!'

'Yeah, we've got to swap addresses and phone numbers,' Philip added. 'Tom does this really cool activity club in the holidays—I want to find out about it.'

'You do an activity club,' Molly pointed out.

'Yeah, but not with *Tom*. Please, Mum?'

She sighed. 'Oh, all right, then, but don't get in the way and hold them up. I want you back here in five minutes, all right?'

She watched them go, then went to check the bedrooms

60

to make sure she had everything. She was down on her hands and knees fishing a pair of socks out from under Philip's bed when a large pair of trainers appeared in her line of sight.

Flustered, her hair on end, she sat back on her heels and pushed the wild tangle out of her eyes. 'Hi,' she said softly.

He sat down on the edge of the bed, just beside her. 'Hi,' he echoed. He looked thoughtful.

'Are the kids with you?' she asked.

He shook his head. 'No. I've left them finishing up the biscuits and orange juice. I expect they'll all be sick on the way home.' He looked down at his hands, his fingers locked together, the knuckles white.

'About us,' he began.

Molly twisted the socks into a knot and hung on tight.

'Molly, it's been wonderful to get to know you—to have some time with you, even if it wasn't enough. It was probably all that was wise, anyway.'

She gave a little laugh and looked up at the ceiling. 'Yes, probably.' Then she screwed up her courage and met his eyes. 'So where do we go from here, Jack?'

'Home,' he said softly. 'I have a book to write to a deadline, the children are busy—just getting through the day takes all the energy and time I have. And you deserve more than that.'

She swallowed hard. 'The children want to see each other again.'

'Yes, I know. They're planning it now. That's fine.'

'But we stay as we are.'

'Yes.' He reached out a hand, and she released her death-grip on the socks and took it. 'I'm sorry, Molly. You'll never know how much. But I just—'

'I understand,' she said, and her voice was astonishingly even and calm. 'You're busy, and so am I. It would be hard to find time to do a relationship justice.'

He stood up and drew her to her feet. 'I'll miss you,' he said gruffly, then he took her mouth in a brief, hard kiss that made her want to cry, and turned away, striding out of the cabin and her life.

She brushed away the tears, fell over Philip's forgotten socks and picked them up, then blew her nose, checked the rooms again and locked up. The children were waiting out by the cars, still chatting to Amy and Tom, and she went over, said goodbye to them all and managed to avoid looking at Jack in case she made a cake of herself.

They all piled in the car and she set off, queuing with the others on the way out of the holiday village, and she managed to get all the way home, unpack the car, get the first load of washing in and retrieve the cat from the cattery up the road before the tears wouldn't be checked.

'I need a bath,' she told the children, and shut herself in the bathroom with a cup of tea, a book and lots of loudly running water while she indulged herself in a really good cry.

It was just a holiday romance, she told herself. They happen all the time. It's a good job he was a gentleman, or you might have been pregnant by now, and even if not, it would have been a lot worse. Just imagine how hard it would be if he'd—if he hadn't stopped. If he'd done the things you wanted—if he'd loved you—

She blew her nose again and sniffed hard, scrubbing her face with a flannel and dragging in a deep breath. She let it out with a hard sigh, grabbed the soap and attacked herself with it, scrubbing and rinsing and towelling herself briskly.

Silly nonsense, she told herself. It was ridiculous getting so worked up. So he'd kissed her. So she'd wanted more. So what? She was an adult, not a teenager to go all moony-eyed over the first half-decent man who'd looked at her in years.

And kissed her.

And called her beautiful.

Oh, God.

She pressed her fingers into her eyes and counted to ten, then wound her hair up in a towel, swooshed water round the bath to rinse it and let herself out of the bathroom.

Cassie and Philip were having a fight in the sitting room over the television, and she went in, wrestled the remote control from them, switched it off and sent them to unpack their bags.

'Welcome home,' she murmured quietly to herself, and went to check the freezer. She had to start work again on Monday, and she'd need to shop tomorrow so she had all her ingredients.

She wasn't sure she could get up at four in the morning any more. Funny how quickly you got out of the routine. It didn't take much. Just a few days away, and dreaming about a man with crinkly eyes and a mouth that could drive her to distraction...

Jack was going mad. The first few days back had been hell. The kids had been flopping about saying they were bored by nine o'clock on Sunday morning, and he was heartily glad to pack them all off to school on the Monday so he could get back to work. Half-term was a blessing and a curse, he thought, but at least the holiday had been a success.

At least, he thought it had. He could hardly remember it now. It seemed to have been submerged in acres of washing and ironing and overlaid by rows about home-work.

Nicky was a bit unsettled, as well, and seemed to have got used to doing without her nap, which did nothing for his writing schedule.

And anyway, he thought, glaring at the screen, what he was writing wasn't worth nuts.

His hero, a scruffy, hard-bitten private investigator, was busy falling in love with his client—a tiny, feisty woman with a tangle of blonde hair and sparkling blue-green eyes.

Funny, before they went on holiday her hair had been straight and dark and her eyes had been brown.

Damn.

He closed his eyes, pushed back the chair and wondered how long he was going to ache for her. Every night he woke from a restless, dream-filled sleep, his arms empty and his body screaming for Molly and the soft heat of her body welcoming him—

'Oh, God, stop it,' he growled, and closed the file, de-clining to save what he'd written. It wasn't worth keeping.

He went out into the garden and attacked a few weeds while the dog lay whining softly by the gate. He sighed and straightened up. 'Want a walk, Boy?' he asked.

The dog stood up and barked, tail lashing furiously, so he washed his hands, grabbed the lead just in case and set off over the fields to the river. It was calm and peaceful there, the soft trickling of the river soothing. It was here he did his best thinking, while Boy snuffled about in the undergrowth and chased rabbits that were much too sly for him.

Today, though, his thinking wasn't about the book at all, but Molly. All he seemed to be able to focus on was the tilt of her mouth, a little too wide, soft and welcoming, the lips slightly parted because she always was about to laugh or speak. He longed to kiss it, to feel the wild and willing response he'd felt before.

Maybe that had been a one-off. Maybe it wouldn't happen again. Perhaps he ought to try, just in case, so he could lay it to rest—

Oh, damn.

He was such a fool. Even he could see through that piece of self-delusion. He headed back up to the house, dried the dog and put him in the utility room, then it was time to fetch Nicky from the day nursery and bring her home for lunch. Please, God, let her need a nap this afternoon, he prayed.

She didn't, and he had a difficult and devious conversation with his editor over the phone with Nicky swarming over his lap and trying to kiss him and grab the phone to say hello.

'If you don't mind me saying so, you could do with a little professional discipline,' the man said drily, and Jack would have laughed if the threat hadn't been all so real.

'I'll try and sort things out. Don't worry, Patrick, it's coming on,' he lied, crossing his fingers behind Nicky's back.

'It had better be. You've only got eight weeks, and I haven't seen the first draft yet.'

'Don't panic,' he said with as much calm as he could muster. 'I'll get there. It's almost done.'

Hah. In his dreams.

He wrestled the phone from Nicky, replaced it on the hook and looked at the little pixie on his lap. 'You are a pest,' he told her affectionately, and hugged her. Pest or not, he wouldn't have been without her—without any of them.

However, that wasn't going to get his book written. 'How about cartoons?' he suggested hopefully.

'Want to make biscuits,' she said round her thumb.

'I can't make biscuits.'

'Molly can. Want Molly.'

And so do I, he thought with almost hysterical desperation. So do I.

'Jack?'

He glanced down at Amy, snuggled up against his side, her head on his shoulder. 'Yes, poppet?'

'Can we have Cassie and Philip over this weekend? Tomorrow, perhaps?'

He stifled the groan. 'Not this weekend, darling. It's a bit busy.'

She straightened and turned to look at him with accusing eyes. 'It isn't! None of us are doing anything! Seb's revising for his exams, Nicky's not going to the party because Luby's got chicken pox, and we weren't doing anything anyway. Besides, you said we could see them again whenever we liked.'

He sighed. So much for forgetting about them all. 'We'll see,' he compromised, but Amy wasn't fooled.

'That means no,' she said flatly.

'It means we'll see,' he corrected. 'They might be busy.'

She scooted off the sofa. 'I'll ring them.'

And before he could protest, she was off, darting away to the study to phone Cassie. He sighed. There were times, he thought, when he felt like King Canute—utterly helpless in the face of the tide of their resolve. They were just relentless.

And he was going to have to see Molly again.

His heart kicked against his ribs, and the dog lifted his head and looked at him strangely. Were the vibes coming off him that strong?

Probably. He stifled a snort of laughter and tried to concentrate on the television, but it was hopeless. Amy ran back in.

'Molly wants to talk to you,' she said breathlessly, hair flying, and he unravelled himself from the chair, went into the study and closed the door firmly. Then he took a deep, steadying breath before picking up the receiver.

'Molly?'

'Hi,' she said, and her voice went straight to his loins and played hell with his concentration. 'About Saturday— I offered to have them here but Amy said something about the barn, and Philip seems desperate to come to you. Are you sure it's all right?'

Six kids, he thought with a mental groan, and found himself agreeing anyway, just so he could talk to her a little longer. 'I'll come and pick them up,' he offered, and knew it was only because he wanted to see her house and be able to picture her in it so he could torture himself better.

'Will they all fit in your car?' she asked, somehow managing to be sensible. 'I know you've got a people carrier, but they don't all have seven seats.'

'Mine's got eight—I seem to spend my life ferrying children, so it seemed a good idea to have the extra seats. Anyway, Seb will stay here, so it's not that bad.'

'Why don't I bring them to you? I feel so guilty,' she protested.

And, he thought, if she brings them, I can talk her into staying for a coffee, and then I can run them back and maybe she'll invite me in and I can indulge my fantasies a little further.

'OK,' he agreed, too hastily, and gave her directions. Then he thought about all the housework he'd have to do before she arrived, and wondered if it was all worth it, just for a few seconds of dubious pleasure that would torture his sleep for weeks.

Molly felt guilty. No only was she off-loading the children tomorrow, but she'd managed to wangle it so she could deliver them to his house and see where he lived. That way she could picture him in it, and her fantasies would have more substance.

What a stupid idea! They were disturbing enough as it was—

'Mummy, are we going to them, or are they coming here?'

'You're going to them,' she told Cassie, and watched in dismay as her daughter bounced out of the sitting room and went to tell Philip. There was a cheer from the other end of the house, and she followed the sound. 'Nobody's going anywhere until this place is tidy, all homework's done and your bedrooms have been cleaned,' she said firmly, and they skittered off upstairs to make a start.

'Perhaps they ought to go to him every weekend,' she murmured drily. 'Such enthusiasm.'

And then she found herself cleaning the bathroom and polishing the dining table and dusting the lampshades.

The morning brought a new dilemma. What should she wear to drop the children off?

Jeans and a T-shirt, as usual, her common sense told her, but it was a lovely day and there was that sundress that brought back so many memories—

She put her jeans on, chastising herself for being so foolish, but she couldn't resist a flick of mascara and a brush of lipstick. Not enough to show, she told herself, just a little touch to hide behind.

'Come on, kids, are you ready?'

They skidded to a halt at her feet. 'Yup,' they said in unison, eyeing her make-up curiously.

'Homework done?'

They nodded.

'Rooms tidy?'

Philip looked a little uncomfortable, but, for some reason she chose not to examine, she couldn't be bothered to argue. 'Come on, then. Let's go,' she said, and bundled them into the car.

It took twenty minutes to get there—mostly because she had sandwiches to drop off on the way. In fact, she thought, if she hadn't called in at the garage it would only have taken about ten to fifteen minutes—nothing, really. She hadn't realised they lived so close together.

The last couple of hundred yards were up a little lane that petered out into a track. A wide white gate, propped open and sagging on its hinges, bore the name Mill House, and she could see the house ahead of them, a white-painted brick house, partly Victorian, partly indeterminate, with a big wooden-sided barn opposite it and the remains of an old mill base just beyond.

A black dog rushed out, tail lashing, followed by Tom and Amy, and as she parked the car and climbed out Jack appeared in the doorway, looking big and solid and very, very tempting.

She was suddenly terribly glad she'd worn her jeans and not the sundress, because even from that distance she could see the heat in his eyes.

She shut the car door, propped her sunglasses in her hair and hoped her smile wasn't too inane. 'Hi,' she called.

'Hi. I've put the kettle on.'

Thank you, God, she thought. Her smile brightened even further. 'Sounds good. It's been a busy morning.'

Liar, her conscience screamed. Once she'd made the order for the garage she'd done nothing but fuss round plumping cushions and brushing the cat! The dog was sniffing her ankles, tail still wagging, and she reached down and patted it.

Jack slapped his thigh. 'Come on, Boy. Inside.' He held his arm out to beckon her in, and after a heartbeat's hesitation, he bent and dropped a chaste kiss on her cheek. 'You look well,' he murmured, and cleared his throat.

'So do you,' she replied, and could have laughed at them. They were so forced, so polite, so civilised, and yet the message in his eyes was a totally different one, and she had a feeling hers were giving just as much away.

'So, how's things?' he asked, fiddling with the kettle.

She sat down, looking round the big farmhouse-style kitchen appreciatively. Their kitchen simply wasn't big enough to eat in, but this one had acres of worktop that she would have given her eye teeth for, and an Aga, and a table and chairs and a sofa that the dog was lying on, head hanging off the edge, eyes watchful.

'Fine,' she told him. 'Monday morning was a bit tough, getting up at four—'

'Four!' he exclaimed. 'Why on earth did you get up at four?'

'To make my sandwiches,' she said, surprised. 'What time did you think I got up?'

He shrugged. 'I don't know—six, maybe?'

She laughed. 'I wouldn't get them all done if I got up at six. By six they're all packaged up, sealed, dated and loaded into trays.'

He put the coffee down on the table and sat opposite her, his eyes searching her face. 'It sounds more serious than I'd realised. I thought you just made a few rolls and delivered them up the road.'

'I wish,' she laughed. 'Well, no, I don't, really, because we just wouldn't survive. No, I get up at four, prepare the fillings and put them all together, then after the kids are off to school I take them up to the industrial estates and sell them.'

'Just on spec?'

She shook her head. 'No—the firms have regular orders, although I do some speculative ones. My last stop's the garage on the main road, and they take a regular order and any leftovers from the industrial estate. The next day I pick up any left from the day before and freeze them for packed lunches, because they have to be sold the day they're made.'

He looked stunned. 'Hell's teeth,' he said softly. 'And I have enough trouble flinging together a few tuna rolls for the kids!'

She chuckled. 'You get used to it. I have a system— and doing large quantities doesn't take a great deal longer. It can get boring, though.'

'Do you do egg ones? How do you mash all the eggs? I hate doing that—they all skid round the bowl.'

'Not in a food processor.'

He grinned. 'Crafty.'

'I make fifty egg and cress sandwiches every morning. I haven't got time to mash them with a fork.'

Again, his eyes widened. 'Fifty?' He pulled a face. 'What other flavours do you do?'

'Tuna and mayonnaise, tuna and cucumber, BLT, chicken tikka, cheese salad, cheese and pickle, chicken salad, ham and salad, Mediterranean salad—that's feta cheese, olives, tomatoes and peppers in lettuce and oil dressing—I don't know, tons.'

'Every day?'

He sounded incredulous. Most people did when they realised it was a serious business.

'Every day,' she confirmed. 'Except Saturday and Sunday. On Saturday and Sunday I just do the garage—that's easy.'

He shook his head. 'I had no idea.'

'No one does.' She watched a bubble circling on her coffee, and blew on it to chase it. 'So how's the book going?'

He snorted. 'Oh, wonderful. Just peachy. I can't—um—the words aren't there.'

'Writer's block?' she said sympathetically, not really having the slightest idea what he was going through.

His smile was wry. 'I think my editor sees that as a fancy name for not getting my nose down to the grindstone with sufficient professional discipline.'

'And is it?' she asked, struggling to trap the smile.

Jack laughed. 'Probably. Whatever, I go to the machine in the morning and, yup, I'm still on the page I was on the night before. I had hoped, after all this practice, that the darned thing could do it itself, but apparently not.'

'Perhaps you've got the wrong model,' she offered helpfully, and then his eyes crinkled and she was lost.

'I'll have to keep coaching it.' He lounged back in the chair, one hand curled around his mug, the other hand stuffed into the pocket of his jeans, drawing her attention to the unconsciously masculine pose.

She buried her nose in the top of her mug and tried to ignore the sight of him sprawled there, so much at home. And it was a home, she knew, a home for the dog, for the ginger cat sitting on the windowsill watching the birds outside, for all the children.

Fridge magnets held reminders and drawings and all the chaos of a family, and there were more paintings on the walls, stuck up with Blutac and signed by the younger children.

Then, framed, was a drawing of a spacecraft, signed Sebastian Selenka.

'Is that Seb's?' she asked, wondering about the surname.

'Yes. They kept their parents' name.'

'Even though you adopted them?'

He nodded. 'Yes. I felt it was right. They are who they are—all I'm doing is acting as guardian of their childhood, making sure no harm befalls them before they grow up. They're still very much their parents' children as well as mine.'

She eyed him curiously.

'Do you ever regret it?'

'No.'

Quick, emphatic, underlined by a sharp shake of the head.

'Even though it must have meant a phenomenal change in lifestyle?'

He laughed ruefully. 'It certainly did. I went from being a divorced and totally unencumbered detective to being married, widowed and the parent of four children, a dog and a cat in the space of less than a year—and I changed my occupation, or at least, it was the spur to make me give up my day job, so to speak.'

'Weren't you scared?'

'Spitless. I had to move, of course—the flat I was in was woefully inadequate, and Jan didn't want to stay in their house in London, so near where Nick was shot, so we all migrated to Suffolk. We found this place, moved all their things in, and Jan settled down to die in peace.'

'Was she here?' Molly asked, curious. The house didn't

have any bad vibes, so if she'd died in it, she'd at least left it peaceful, but Jack was shaking his head.

'In the end, no. She went into the hospice for the last few days, but by then she didn't know anybody, so really, I suppose, she was here when the thing that made her who she was faded away.'

Molly shook her head. 'It must have been horrendous.'

'Not—horrendous. Very gentle, really. We were all left just empty, cast adrift. It was most odd. But very sad, yes. We all cried for what seemed like ages—all except Seb. He didn't—not for weeks. When he cracked, he really fell apart. I was very worried about him.'

What a huge responsibility, she thought. Fancy having to deal with all of that alone. He must have huge strength of character.

And who, she wondered, had comforted him?

Nobody, of course.

How very, very sad.

She cleared her throat and looked at her watch. 'Good grief, is that the time? I promised a friend I'd go shopping,' she lied, and got to her feet. 'What time shall I pick them up?'

'I'll drop them back—I've got the address; I know more or less where you are. No doubt the kids will know once I get close enough.'

'Thanks—if you're sure you don't mind? Kick them out as soon as you're sick of them. I'll be at home from two.'

'How about six?' he suggested.

'Sure?'

He nodded. 'They're no trouble. I think the girls are in the garden with Nicky, and I expect the boys have disappeared into the barn. I'll bring them back at six.'

She left, watching him in the rearview mirror, and

waved to the boys through the window in the top of the barn. She hoped it was safe. They looked a long way up. Still, Jack wouldn't let anything happen to them.

'Molly?'

'Oh, hi, Jack. I was expecting you any minute. Do you want me to come instead?'

'Um—not exactly. Look, Molly, I've got a problem. I can't find the boys.'

She sat down, her heart giving a sudden and violent thump. 'What?' she squeaked. 'When did you last see them?'

'I don't know. Two, maybe? After lunch. They were pestering Seb, but he's gone off on his bike to a friend's house, and the girls are baking with Nicky, and there's no sign of them. I don't suppose you could come over and give me a hand to look?'

She could hear the desperation in his voice, and, even though she knew they were very probably quite all right, she could imagine the scenarios running through his mind. After all, he'd been a detective. He must have seen some grisly things—

'Oh, God, no,' she moaned, and then forced herself to get a grip. 'I'll come now. Keep looking. I'll be with you in fifteen minutes—and Jack?'

'Yes?'

'When you find them, thrash them.'

He gave a startled laugh. 'Don't worry, I will,' he said grimly, and put the phone down.

She grabbed her bag and keys, shut the house and ran out of the front, slamming the door and jumping into her car. Her key wouldn't go into the ignition lock, and she forced herself to slow down and breathe calmly. 'Take it steady,' she told herself. 'You having an accident won't help at all.' She drove carefully, consciously slowing down and running on adrenaline.

Even so, she arrived there in a little under fifteen minutes, to find Jack on the drive waiting for her.

She skidded to a halt and jumped out. 'Have you found them?'

'No. I've looked everywhere. Well, almost. There's a gravel pit—'

'Oh, God.' She felt the blood drain from her face and clutched at the car for support. 'Does it flood?'

He nodded. 'But they can both swim.'

'What about the cold?'

'Molly, it's June. The water's not that cold. They're just messing around somewhere.'

She swung round, scanning the landscape as if she really expected them to jump out from behind a bush. 'You've checked the barn?'

He sighed shortly. 'Yes, I've checked the barn—three times. They aren't there. I heard some scuffling, but nothing bigger than a mouse.'

'Where are the girls?' she asked, panic rising again.

'Inside, with Nicky.'

She took a steadying breath. 'Right. OK. Where does Tom go to play?'

Jack shrugged. 'The barn?'

'But you said they were annoying Seb. Where was he?'

'In the house.'

'And have you searched the house?'

He looked at her as if she was quite mad. 'The house? Where would they be in the house?'

'I don't know,' Molly snapped, worried to death. 'The attic? The cellar?'

Jack's face registered surprise. 'The cellar—I forgot all

about it. But they never go down there; no one does. It's dank and nasty, and we never use it.'

'And that, of course, makes it a perfect place for little boys to play.'

'My God.'

'Jump in, we'll go in the car, it's quicker.'

She started the engine as Jack folded himself in beside her and slammed the door. She shot up the drive in a great splatter of gravel, and skidded to a halt by the front door. Before she'd turned off the engine Jack was out of the car and heading inside, and she followed him in at a run.

'Tom? Philip?' he was yelling, and from beneath their feet came a muffled reply.

Jack's shoulders sagged, and, running into the dining room, he rolled back the rug, pulled up a trapdoor and flicked on a light switch. 'Boys?' he called.

'Down here,' Tom replied, and Jack went carefully down the stairs and crouched down below the low ceiling. Molly followed him, ducking to avoid the rafters, and shivered with the cold.

'They're here,' he said gruffly, and she knelt down beside him and put her arms around Philip.

'Darling, whatever are you doing down here?' she asked, trying to quell the hysteria.

Both boys stayed mutinously silent, their tear-stained faces pale in the yellow light, their eyes like saucers.

'They're tied up,' Jack growled under his breath. 'I'll kill Seb.'

'It wasn't his fault!' Tom protested tearfully. 'We made him play with us.'

'It was meant to be a dungeon—he was going to hang us in the morning if we made any noise,' Philip added.

Jack loosened the bonds and the boys got stiffly to their feet, rubbing their wrists and ankles wretchedly. They were shivering, and Jack's face was like thunder. He followed the boys up, leaving Molly to follow, and led them into the kitchen.

'Hot soup,' he said firmly, and pushed them down onto the sofa with the dog.

Molly knelt down in front of them and took their hands, looking at their wrists. They looked a little sore, but the skin wasn't broken and all in all they seemed all right. She sat back on her heels.

'So you were supposed to be Seb's prisoners, were you?' she said, her calm returning.

'Yeah—we were in the Tower of London, and we'd been caught trying to blow up the Houses of Parliament,' Philip explained.

'Seb's revising history for an exam,' Jack said tightly. 'His plot, no doubt.' He poured the hot soup into mugs, pressed them into the boys' hands, and went into the study. A moment later he came out.

'Sebastian's on his way home,' he growled. 'We'll see what he has to say for himself.'

Molly looked at his thunderous face and felt suddenly terribly sorry for Seb. She had a feeling the forthcoming interview with Jack would be more than somewhat chastening, and she wouldn't be in his shoes for anything...

CHAPTER FIVE

SEB arrived back a few moments later, threw his bike in the barn and came in, grinding to a halt on the doorstep.

'You—in the study,' Jack said shortly, and the boy went past him, head up, a mutinous expression on his face, throwing the younger boys a dirty look on the way past.

Molly laid a hand on Jack's arm. 'Don't thrash him,' she murmured.

He gave a tight smile. 'Only with my tongue.'

He followed Seb through the kitchen, through the snug and into the study, closing the door with an ominous click. There was a low rumble, then Seb's voice raised, then another rumble, Seb again, louder this time, then a roar that made the windows rattle.

Molly closed the kitchen door softly and turned to the boys. 'Are you all right now? Warming up?'

They nodded, but Tom had tears in his eyes. 'He'll kill us,' he whispered.

'I don't think so—not when Jack's finished with him.' The roar had subsided to a steady rumble, punctuated by the occasional protest from Seb. The door opened at the other end of the kitchen, and the girls came in.

'You found the boys, then,' Amy said, unconcerned.

'Yes, we did,' Molly told them. 'They're fine—they were in the cellar.'

'The *cellar*!'

'Seb tied us up,' Tom told her.

Amy's eyes boggled. 'Is that what the fuss is about? We heard Jack yell—oh, cripes.'

'He's—ah—talking to Seb now,' Molly said diplomatically. 'So, what have you girls been up to in the meantime?'

'We've dressed Nicky up,' Cassie said, and produced her from behind them. It reminded Molly of the magic act with the rabbit, only a little slicker than hers had been. She smiled. Nicky's blonde hair was tied up in bows all over her head, and she had dolly make-up on, red cheeks and blue eyes and too much lipstick.

'Doesn't she look cute?' Amy said with satisfaction. 'We used Mum's make-up. She gave it to me years ago for dressing up and I'd forgotten I had it. Nicky, do a twirl.'

She took the little girl and turned her round, and she nearly tripped over in the huge old court shoes. Molly stifled a smile.

'You look lovely, Nicky. Really cute.'

'Nicky got make-up,' Nicky said proudly.

'I see.' Molly bit her cheeks and looked away for a moment, but Cassie caught her eye and giggled.

Molly smiled. 'Just don't get it on the walls or the furnishings, that's all.' Then Jack's voice roared again, just for a second, and they all froze.

'He's really mad,' Tom said in awe. 'He just never shouts.'

Molly dragged in a deep breath and looked around. 'Um—how about a cup of tea?'

'I'm starving,' Philip said, and Tom nodded.

'Me, too. When are we going to have supper?'

She looked at them all. 'What was going to be for supper, do you know?'

Amy shrugged. 'Jack usually consults the freezer,' she said, obviously quoting him. 'It's in the little barn.'

'Where's that?'

'Through the study.'

Six pairs of eyes swivelled to the study door. 'Ah,' Molly said. 'I wonder what's in the fridge?'

She opened it and pulled out cheese, eggs, milk, margarine, some ham that was inside its sell-by date, and a few tomatoes. 'How about quiche?' she suggested, and they nodded.

'Mum makes really nice quiche,' Cassie told them.

'My mum used to make really nice quiche, too,' Amy said quietly.

Oh, lawks, Molly thought, is it like this all the time, with every conversation a minefield? 'I don't know if my quiche will be as nice as hers—I tell you what, why don't you all help? Boys, can you find a mixing bowl? Girls, I want flour, a rolling pin and the cheese grater.'

'Me help,' Nicky said, raising her arms, and Molly lifted her up, bows, lipstick and all, and sat her down on the worktop. The shoes fell off with a plop and an echo, and Nicky looked expectantly at her.

'You can tear the ham into little bits,' she told the child, and gave her the packet to shred. 'Amy, what about the oven?'

'The Aga's off—Jack uses that one.'

She pointed at an electric oven set into the units. Molly turned it on, relieved that it was a straightforward fan oven similar to her own, and turned back to the troops. 'Right, guys, how are we doing? Found that bowl yet?'

The bowl appeared, they all washed their hands and then Molly smiled at them.

'Right, let's make the best quiche in Suffolk, shall we?'

They weighed the margarine, sifted the flour, kneaded

and rolled, beat and sliced and shredded and chopped and filled the case, popped it in the oven, cleared up the kitchen and sat back to wait.

The tantalising smell was just starting to waft through the kitchen when they heard the study door open, then the door from the snug. Seb, looking pale and chastened and obviously holding back tears, came quietly out.

'I'm sorry, Tom, Philip,' he said, a little hoarsely. 'I didn't mean to scare you. I forgot I'd tied you up.' He turned to Molly. 'I'm sorry I scared you, too. I promise I won't ever do anything like that again.'

He dragged his eyes up to hers, and she saw genuine remorse in them. 'I know you won't,' she said softly. 'It's all right, Seb, there's no real harm done.'

He swallowed, nodded and walked swiftly across the room, ran up the stairs and closed his bedroom door behind him with a muted click. Molly looked up at Jack, standing in the doorway. 'All right?' she asked.

He nodded. 'Sorry, boys. Are you all OK?'

'We're fine—Molly helped us make quiche for supper, 'cos we were starving,' Tom told him, bouncing back with all the natural resilience of youth.

His eyes locked with Molly's, and she lifted her shoulders. 'We needed to do something, and they were hungry. I hope it's OK.'

He shot her a crooked smile. 'It's fine. Bless you. I take it you're staying to eat with us?'

'Well—we weren't,' she began, but the howls of protest from the children drowned her out.

'Please,' Jack said softly.

She crumbled. 'All right, then. Thank you, that would be lovely—especially if you've got a microwave and a few big potatoes I can bake.'

'Sure. Amy, could you and Cassie make a salad, please, and Nicky—good grief, whatever's happened to Nicky?'

His face was so comical it broke the tension, and they all started to laugh.

'Not funny!' Nicky cried, and Jack scooped her up and hugged her, oblivious to the lipstick being smeared all over his cheeks.

'No, sweetheart, it's not, I'm sorry. You look beautiful.' He held her at arm's length, studied her and grinned crookedly. 'Absolutely gorgeous. Right, you lot, jump to it; I'm starving. Let's get this show on the road.'

'Thanks for cooking supper and staying with us—it softened it all a bit for the boys.'

Molly nodded. 'You won't be too harsh on him, will you?' she pleaded.

Jack shook his head. 'No. He's grounded until after his exams, he has extra jobs to do in the house and he's been denied access to the phone for a month. Apart from that, and a little chat to point out the error of his ways, he's emerged unscathed, which is more than the young scamp deserved.'

Molly smiled at him and sipped her coffee. They were sitting in the kitchen, on the doggy sofa, the ginger cat was curled up in Jack's lap and the children were watching television in the snug. Seb was still in his room, having had a small supper taken up to him on a tray by Jack after they'd all finished, and Nicky was tucked up in bed, finally free of all but the last trace of lipstick.

'Peaceful,' Molly murmured, dropping her head back against the sofa and sighing contentedly.

'I'm sorry I dragged you out on such a wild-goose chase. Thank goodness you thought of the cellar.'

'I just thought of my childhood. I used to go into all

the nasty, creepy, odd places to scare myself a little—but I doubt if even I would have wanted to play down there.'

He shuddered. 'I hate small confined spaces. I usually walk up stairs rather than go for the lift.'

Something about the way he said it alerted her. She looked at him closely. 'What happened?' she murmured.

He said nothing for a moment, then gave her a crooked smile. 'I got a little close to the action once. Someone decided I'd be better out of the way, so they bundled me into a safe.'

'A safe? What, a bank vault?'

'No, a safe,' he corrected. 'A large one. I could almost sit up in it. There wasn't a lot of air.'

He dragged in a deep breath, and straightened up, as if trying to overwhelm the image. His voice had been quiet and level, but there was no doubt that the memory was all too clear.

'What happened?'

'Nick worked out where I must be, and they cracked the combination and got me out just in time. He used one of his informers—a sneaky, evil piece of work, but I was never so glad to see anyone in my life!'

'What happened to the person who shut you in?'

He shrugged. 'He's tucked up out of the way, costing the taxpayers a fortune. He'll be out in a few years, and no doubt he's already planning the next heist.'

He glanced at his watch. 'It's nearly nine-thirty—I ought to get these two to bed.'

She leapt up. 'Oh, I'm so sorry—I had no idea it was so late! Fancy overstaying our welcome like that—'

'You could never overstay your welcome,' he said quietly, and she stopped flustering and looked up into his eyes. His hands, big and warm and gentle, cupped her cheeks, and he lowered his head and brushed her lips with his. 'Thanks for being here, for getting the supper. I'm sorry about Seb.'

'Don't be too hard on him, Jack,' she pleaded. 'Nobody's been hurt, everybody's learned something and no real harm's been done.'

'Apart from the ten years he took off my life,' Jack growled softly, but she could tell it was all bluster. Seb was safe, if chastened, and Jack would make sure the lesson was well learned.

She rounded up the children, said their goodbyes and shooed them out to the car, made sure their seatbelts were fastened and drove off, waving and calling goodbye.

The children toppled into bed exhausted, Philip particularly, and she followed soon after. She had to be up early, after all, and it was already nearly ten.

Besides, she was exhausted from the emotion of the day. She was asleep as soon as her head hit the pillow, but her sleep was troubled, disturbed by dreams of cellars and dungeons, and once she woke drenched with sweat, convinced she was locked into a safe.

She rolled onto her back, stared at the ceiling and made herself breathe nice and evenly until the panic passed. It was difficult, and she wondered again what kind of man Jack was to have survived such a terrifying ordeal.

She thought of the way he'd dealt with Seb, then the things he'd said during supper, and finally the kiss, soft and undemanding, just a touch of his lips against hers.

She wanted more. She wanted to hold him, and comfort him, and give him back some of the things he gave to others, the kindness, the support, the love.

Especially the love...

Jack woke suddenly, heart pounding, his body drenched with sweat. Instantly, without thinking, he stretched out all his limbs, feeling for the walls, breath locked in his chest by an iron band of panic.

'Oh, God,' he groaned, relief flooding him, and throwing aside the bedclothes he went over to the window, threw it wide and dragged the cool, clean air into his tortured lungs.

He'd thought it was over—thought the dreams were finished with. Talking to Molly, finding the boys locked in that dark and terrifying place, must have brought it all back.

He wondered how the children were, if their dreams were tormented by the same sort of fear as his, but he thought probably not. The cellar, although dark and gloomy, did have a tiny window high up on the outside wall, and there was a constant supply of fresh air from a vent. They'd also known that Seb would come back and let them out.

It was hardly the same as being locked in a safe and left to die.

He dragged air in again, staring out over the lightening horizon, his thoughts turning to Molly. She'd been brilliant last night, taking the kids' minds off their ordeal, feeding them all without fuss or bother, taking it all in her stride.

She'd make a wonderful wife, he thought, and then slammed on the brakes.

You're a fool, Haddon, he told himself. Just a bloody fool. No woman in her right mind would take on a broken-down old cop with four kids. Forget it. Forget Molly.

He left the curtains open and the window wide, and lay down again in his bed, arms folded behind his head, staring out at the dawn.

He couldn't forget Molly. It wasn't that easy. She warmed him with her kindness and humour, he admired her sense of fair play and genuine liking for the children, and his body craved hers in a way he'd never experienced before.

He felt driven by need, almost overwhelmed by the urge to contact her, to call her on an hourly basis just to hear her voice.

He hadn't done it, hadn't indulged himself—well, not until yesterday. Then he'd thrown away his common sense, invited her in for coffee and sat drooling over her for as long as he'd been able to keep her there.

Then the fates had conspired to call her back in the evening to help search for the boys, and had kept her by his side until after nine o'clock.

And now, alone in his bed for yet one more dawn in the endless wasteland of his personal life, he ached for her. His arms felt empty, his lips cold, the rest of him too hot. He closed his eyes and groaned. It was madness. She wasn't the sort of woman he could dally with, take to bed and keep in a compartment labelled 'Recreation'.

He didn't want to. He wanted to spend every minute of every day with her, but he knew it was just the white heat of lust. Of course it was. And she was a lovely person, which made his urges easier to justify.

And impossible to act on.

He swore softly, turned his head into the pillow and smashed it into shape, rammed it back under his head and shut his eyes.

It didn't work. Five minutes later he'd tugged on his jeans, let the dog out and was sitting in his study, watching the cursor on the computer screen blip gently on his last word, and wondering how the hell he was going to dredge up sufficient concentration to finish the book.

'Mummy, please can they come round for the day?'

Molly paused, spreading the filling in a sandwich, and

looked at Cassie in the doorway behind her. 'I've got a
lot to do today—I've got to drop these sandwiches off
and start the buffet for tonight—I don't have time to run
around after you all.'

'But we wouldn't be any trouble,' her daughter reasoned. 'Tom and Philip would play in the garden, and
Amy and I can paint or make dolls' clothes for Nicky or
something. *Pleeeeeese*, Mummy?'

She glanced at the clock on the wall of the sandwich
kitchen. It was only eight o'clock—too early to phone.

'We can't ring them yet.'

'Why not? Jack gets up early every morning to let the
dog out and write his book. He'll be up, you could ring
him—please, Mummy? We haven't seen them for weeks!'

Three weeks, to be exact, all bar thirteen hours. Oh,
blast. 'Let me finish these and I'll ring—perhaps he can
drop them off after I've done the garage order. But if he
can't, I'm sorry, I haven't got time to fetch them; you'll
have to play with Angie and Ben.'

'We always play with Angie and Ben. Angie's boring—she's younger than me and she doesn't like the same
things.'

Molly sighed inwardly. 'I'll ring later. Go on, now,
leave me in peace. Go and do your homework and tidy
your bedroom.'

'Done it.'

'Not your bedroom; I know that. I wasn't born yesterday.'

Cassie huffed and stomped off, the door closing behind
her with a little bang. Alone in her sandwich kitchen, a
sacrosanct space of gleaming worktops and colour-coded
chopping boards each dedicated to a particular food, with

her powerful food-processor in one corner and the packaging equipment in the other, Molly sighed.

She missed him. Crazy though it was, he filled all her waking hours and most of her sleep. She'd thought not seeing him would help to lessen the ache, but it seemed just as strong each day—and the nights were getting worse. Last night, for instance—

Heat brushed her cheeks. She wouldn't think about the dream she'd had last night or she wouldn't be able to talk to him coherently this morning.

Her heart skittered a little with the thought, and anticipation lent wings to her fingers. She finished the sandwiches, wrapped and sealed them, labelled the packets and packed them into the trays, then took them through to the hall. 'Kids, come on, I have to go to the garage.'

'Phone Jack,' Cassie pleaded, bouncing down the stairs. Tom skidded to a halt behind his sister.

'Go on, Mum. He'll think we're still mad with Seb.'

'No, he won't,' she assured them. 'I ought to do this first—'

'It won't take a moment.' Cassie grabbed her arm and dragged her into the sitting room. 'Ring him, Mummy, please!'

So she dialled the number and took a steadying breath.

'Haddon.'

He sounded preoccupied and cross, and Molly swallowed. 'Jack, it's Molly.'

'Molly—hi.' His voice softened, suddenly husky, and her heart skittered again. 'How are you all?'

'Fine—um, look, the kids wondered if Amy and Tom were busy today. I've got to do a wedding buffet for this evening, so I'm stuck here, but if you were able to bring them over, it would do me a huge favour. They could help entertain mine and keep them out of mischief, and I could drop them back later. I'll feed them, if you like, first—'

She shut her mouth fast before she gabbled any more, and waited.

'Jack?'

'I'm still here—sorry, I was thinking. Yes, that's fine; I'm sure they'll be delighted. We'll come in a few minutes, if that's OK?'

'Give me half an hour,' she said. 'I have to go to the garage with these sandwiches.'

'OK. I'll see you later.'

'Great. Thanks, Jack.'

She cradled the phone, wiped the silly grin off her face and turned back to the children. 'He's bringing them in a while. Right, into the car, let's do this delivery and pick up something nice for lunch.'

Jack cradled the phone softly and sat back, closing his eyes. Lord, her voice. It did terminal things to his innards, curling round inside him and leaving a trail of havoc in its wake. His blood pressure must surely have rocketed to dangerous levels, and there was no way his heartbeat was normal.

There was also the stupid smile that he couldn't seem to get rid of.

First things first, though. He went out of the study and found Nicky playing in a pool of something green and slimy on the kitchen floor.

'I washin' the floor,' she said cheerfully. 'See.'

She held up one sticky little hand, and his heart sank. Washing-up liquid, spread all over the floor tiles and making the place an ice rink.

He plucked her out of the puddle, washed her hands and face in the sink and dried her, then parked a chair over the deathtrap and carried her upstairs. Amy was in her bedroom, Tom was sitting on her bed watching her tidy up, and Seb was nowhere to be seen.

'Where's Seb?' he asked.

'In the attic. He says it's the only place he gets any peace.'

Jack put Nicky on the bed next to her brother. 'Watch her,' he commanded, and then went out. 'Seb?'

There was a clattering on the stairs that led from the attic down into Seb's bedroom, and he appeared in the doorway. 'Yes?'

'Want to earn some money?'

Seb looked instantly wary. 'Doing what?'

'Babysitting Nicky for me after we get back from Molly's. I'm just going to drop the other two off there and come back, then I really need to write.'

'Ten quid.'

'Five—and you can use the phone again.'

He hesitated, then nodded. 'OK—but only for the morning.'

'No. Ten-thirty to three. That's my final offer.'

Seb sighed. 'All right, then—but she'd better be good.'

'Or what? You'll tie her up in the cellar?'

Jack turned on his heel and went back to the others. 'Right, you're going to Molly's for the day.'

They shot to their feet, whooping with delight, and Nicky clapped her hands. 'Go Molly's!' she said happily. 'Like Molly.'

'You're coming back to play with Seb,' he said, and Nicky's face crumpled.

'Want Molly!' she cried.

Jack scooped her up. 'You and me both, poppet,' he murmured in her ear. 'You and me both.'

*   *   *

They were hardly back before Jack's big people-carrier drew up outside and they all piled out. Tom and Amy came screeching up the path and thundered on the door, and if Molly hadn't been watching for them, she'd have thought there was a fire.

'Hi, guys,' she said, opening the door, and they grinned at her. 'Come on in.' She met Jack's eyes over their heads, and her heart thumped against her ribs. 'Hi. Come in. Got time for a coffee?'

'Have you?'

His voice was deep and husky and scraped over her nerve-endings, making them tingle. 'I'll make time,' she said with a smile that was probably inane.

'In that case, thanks, coffee would be lovely.'

He followed her into the sitting room, Nicky at his side, and Molly bent down to her. 'Nicky, would you like a drink?'

'Juice, please,' she said, and smiled a smile that threatened to melt Molly's already soft heart.

'I've got some biscuits, too. Let's go and see what we can find.' And, reaching for the little hand, she led her through to the kitchen. Jack followed, looking round him at the house, taking in the surroundings. Everything was clean and tidy, but Molly was well aware that most of the things were well past their sell-by date.

The lounge suite was old and tired, the dining table had come from a sale room, the carpets were worn, but at least they were paid for, and everyone in her family was fed and clothed and housed.

'It's nothing special,' she said defensively.

'It's nice—homely. It reflects you.'

She laughed. 'It would reflect me better if I could afford to buy what I wanted.'

'But you can't, and so you've made it work for you. That's much harder.'

The kitchen was tiny, and he seemed to fill it. She put the kettle on and found Nicky a drink, then caught him looking round in puzzlement.

'It's nothing like your kitchen,' she said, anticipating his reaction.

'It's nothing like I expected, either. How on earth do you manage to make all those sandwiches in here?' he asked, sounding bemused. 'You haven't got any worktop space!'

She chuckled. 'I don't—I wouldn't get a licence to make them in here. I have a special room.' She opened the door at the end of the kitchen and showed him her production-line kitchen. 'This is where it all happens.'

He looked round at the packaging equipment, with the heat sealer and label printer and all the colour-coded equipment, and whistled softly. 'It really is a serious business, isn't it?'

She laughed again, a little wryly. 'Oh, yes. I have to have it inspected regularly, and they do spot checks to make sure I'm not culturing listeria and salmonella in the nooks and crannies.'

She tipped her head and looked at him. 'Can you use sandwiches for the kids? I have to take back any that are unsold, and on some days that's quite a few. I fling them in the freezer but they only keep so long, and the salad ones, of course, can't be frozen at all, and if I can't use them I have to chuck them out. They're fine if you eat them the next day. Any use?'

He nodded. 'Sounds great. The kids would love it—much more variety than they get from me. I'll pay you for them, of course.'

She shook her head. 'Oh, no. I'm not allowed to sell

them. I have to throw them out or eat them myself, but I can't eat that many! You'd be doing me a favour.'

He smiled tentatively. 'OK. Thanks. Ring if you have any and I'll pick them up.'

'Or I'll drop them off. That's easier, because I won't know when I'll have them.'

The kettle clicked off, and she hustled him out of her little factory and made the coffee. Nicky had wandered off to find the others, clutching her biscuits, and they were suddenly alone in the little kitchen.

Awareness throbbed between them, bringing colour to her cheeks and taking the strength from her legs. 'How's Seb?' she asked, casting round for a neutral topic.

'Oh, I think I did the trick. He complained they were pestering him, that Tom always pesters him, and I pointed out that Seb was a link with his father and it was natural that Tom should look up to him. I don't think he'd seen it quite that way before.'

'And has he been good?'

Jack gave a crooked grin. 'Fairly. He's bored, of course. Being grounded is hard for him, he's used to being independent, but he's learned a lesson. He's babysitting Nicky for me today, in fact.'

Molly's eyes widened. 'Will they be all right?'

He chuckled. 'Don't worry, I'll frisk him for string and take away his shoelaces before I leave them alone together.'

Molly laughed with him, her eyes meeting his, and suddenly the laughter drained away, leaving a breathless yearning in its wake.

Jack stopped in his tracks, his eyes locked with hers, and with a muffled oath he put his coffee down and reached for her, just as Tom and Philip came roaring in from the garden.

'Hi—Mum, any biscuits? We're *starving*.'

Jack's mouth tilted in a wry smile, and Molly stepped back, dredged up a smile of her own and turned away. 'Here—don't eat them all. Go and share them with the girls.'

'I want a drink, too—Tom, do you want a drink?'

And the moment was lost. She poured drinks, called the girls, settled an argument about the number of biscuits they could have each and met Jack's eyes over their heads.

She saw longing and frustration and resignation in their depths, and knew her own must look the same. She forced a smile. 'I'll drop them back later,' she said, and he nodded and left, gathering Nicky up on the way.

As the door closed behind them, with a soft click hardly audible above the hubbub of the children, the house seemed suddenly—ridiculously—empty.

CHAPTER SIX

IT WAS amazing, Molly thought, how often she seemed to make too many chicken tikka salad and egg and cress sandwiches once she knew they were Jack's favourites!

She dropped them off at lunchtime two or three times a week, and usually ended up staying for lunch with him. It messed up her scheduling, and she found herself shopping more on the other days and occasionally running out of ingredients because she'd left her brain behind or been in too much of a hurry in the supermarket.

Nicky grew attached to her, and she found the little girl quite irresistible. She'd always adored young children and had planned to have more, but David had soon put paid to that idea. So she was happy to entertain Nicky over lunch while Jack sat slumped in the corner of the sofa and looked exhausted.

'You're burning the candle at both ends, aren't you?' she said to him one day, eyeing him in concern.

'Just trying to fit it all in. My editor's getting nervous about the deadline.'

'And you? Are you getting nervous?'

He closed his eyes and laughed without humour. 'Oh, yes. Oh, Lord, yes. It just seems to have a mind of its own.'

She smiled encouragingly. 'You'll get done. Let me know if I can help.'

'I will.'

'I'll go now, to let you get on. Nicky's looking sleepy.'

He snorted. 'It won't last long enough for a nap—it

96

never does, these days. The afternoons are a bit of a disaster, really, aren't they, darling?'

'Afternoons a 'zaster,' Nicky said with a grin, swarming onto his lap. 'Nicky's a pest.'

He laughed and hugged her. 'I love you, though.'

'Love you,' she chirruped. She gave him a smacking
kiss on the lips and he ruffled her hair and chuckled.

Molly stood up, swallowing the lump in her throat.
What she wouldn't give to be part of this family, but the
thought of six children was too hideous to contemplate.
Anyway, he hadn't asked her.

'Must go. See you soon,' she promised, and let herself
out hastily, driving away without looking back.

Till the end. He was standing by the door, Nicky in his
arms, one hand raised in farewell.

Oh, blast.

Jack knew it was stupid. It was probably the stupidest
thing he'd done in ages, but he missed her. She hadn't
been round with sandwiches for over a week, and he told
himself it was natural concern.

'So ring her,' he muttered, but that wasn't what he
wanted. He knew where she shopped, he'd seen the bags,
heard her talk about it. He knew her schedule, and so,
with military precision, he arranged for Nicky to stay
longer at the childminder's, set off so that he arrived before Molly, and lay in wait in the coffee shop, watching
the car park entrance with eyes like a hawk.

She came in, on time and looking tired and defeated,
and he gave her five minutes, grabbed a basket and started
cruising up and down the aisles.

One aisle caught his eye, and amongst the few bogus
purchases he'd made, he threw in something totally un-
scheduled.

Just in case.

Not that he had any real plans, but it wouldn't hurt to be prepared.

Oh, Lord.

He went through the checkout, timing it so that he emerged just as she wheeled her trolley past.

'Molly!'

Her head jerked up and she slammed on the brakes, causing the person behind to cannon into her. The resulting confusion gave Jack a chance to get close to her, to make sure she was all right.

She was, and she couldn't seem to keep the smile off her face, although she was trying.

'You OK?' he asked softly.

'Yes—fine!' she said breathlessly, and just smiled at him. 'What are you doing here?'

He hefted the bags. 'Shopping,' he lied.

'Oh. Well—hi!' She smiled again, that wonderful smile that used her entire face and dimmed the sun.

His heart thudded.

'Have you finished?' he asked, knowing she had.

She nodded. 'Yes—have you?'

'Yes—I just picked up a few things I'd forgotten, nothing much.' He thought of the contents of the bag, and felt heat rising up his neck. 'Um—how about a cup of tea?'

She looked doubtfully at her trolley. 'I shouldn't—I've got frozen stuff in here.' She brightened. 'I tell you what, why don't you come to mine? The kids have got a club after school, so I don't have to pick them up until four-thirty. Then you could help me carry in the shopping,' she teased.

And we'll be alone. Oh, Lord. 'Thought there was a catch,' he said, wondering if his eyes were giving him away. 'I'll meet you there.'

They split up, going to different ends of the car park, and he waited until he saw her pull out before following her. While he waited, he rummaged in the shopping, transferring one of his purchases into his wallet. Just in case...

She must be mad. Fancy inviting him back here. The place was a tip, the kitchen needed sorting, the bed wasn't made—and what did that have to do with the price of fish? she thought, stopping in her tracks. But just in case...

She ran upstairs anyway, dropped a bag of toiletries and suchlike into the bathroom, yanked up the quilt on her bed and ran down again, arriving in the hall just as he came up the path.

'Hi. Right, you go and put the kettle on, I'll start ferrying this lot in.'

'I've got a better idea,' he said, taking her shoulders and turning her round. 'I'll carry shopping, you put the kettle on and file the stuff in the kitchen.'

She went, throwing Philip's trainers out of the way, picking up a discarded shirt and stuffing it in the washing machine, putting the breakfast things in the dishwasher—

'Where do you want this?'

She straightened up. 'Oh, in the sandwich kitchen—almost all of it. Here.'

She took a bag from him, went through and started packing things away into the fridge. By the time she came out, he'd brought the rest of the things in and was gazing in amazement at the number of loaves she had stacked up.

'Is that just for tomorrow?' he asked incredulously.

'Yes.'

'Good grief.'

'It doesn't go far. Right, come on, tea.'

She put the kettle on, fished a couple of mugs down from the cupboard and turned round—smack into his chest.

'Sorry! I didn't realise you were so...' she hesitated '...close,' she finished softly.

He took the mugs from her hand, set them down on the worktop behind her and drew her into his arms.

'I've missed you, Molly,' he murmured into her hair, and she buried her nose in his shirt and breathed in the heady scent.

'I've missed you, too,' she mumbled through the shirt. She tipped her head back and met his eyes. 'I thought—it's too complicated.'

'I know.'

They stood there for an age, just staring into each other's eyes, then Molly made a decision. It was probably the stupidest thing she'd ever done in her life, right up there with eating worms when she was six and marrying David, but whatever it was, it was stronger than her, and she couldn't fight it any more.

'It doesn't have to be,' she said. 'Too complicated, that is. We could keep it in its place—just our time, for us. Just—every now and again. To keep us sane.'

He swallowed hard. 'Oh, God, Molly, I swore I wouldn't do this,' he whispered.

'Me, too.'

'I even bought condoms today,' he confessed.

She laughed. 'So did I.'

'You did?'

She shrugged. 'I couldn't fight it any more, Jack. I need you.'

His eyes darkened, and he drew her into his arms with a ragged sigh. 'Oh, sweetheart. Oh, Molly, I need you, too—so much.'

She laid her head on his chest, and under her ear she could hear his heart pounding. It was a wonder she could, over the thundering of her own heart. She swallowed and eased away from him.

'Do you want tea?'

He touched her cheek with his hand, just lightly. His thumb grazed her lips, dragging the soft skin. His eyes watched them, hooded and unreadable, and then flickered shut. His jaw worked.

'No,' he said gruffly. 'No, I don't want tea.'

She stepped away and took his hand, leading him upstairs. She made a brief detour to the bathroom for her purchase, then went on, her courage ebbing with every step so that by the time they reached the bedroom, she was wondering if she could go through with this.

She looked round at the hastily tidied room, and swallowed. 'If I'd known, I'd have changed the sheets—'

'Molly, stop it.'

She closed her eyes, trying to quell the panic. What if he found her boring? David had. Oh, Lord, how had she got herself into this mess?

'Molly?'

His voice was soft and close, and his hands cupped her cheeks and tilted her head up to meet his eyes. 'What's wrong?'

She shrugged miserably. 'I want this to work,' she said eventually, her voice uneven. 'I'm just afraid it won't.'

'There's nothing to work or not work, Molly. It's not a production line or a competition. I just want to hold you—touch you. I need to be with you.'

'I'll disappoint you.'

He gave a strangled laugh. 'I don't think so, sweetheart. Not in this lifetime.'

She bowed her head. 'David said—'

'I'm not David, Molly. This is me—boring old Jack.'

Her head flew up. 'You're not boring!'

'My wife said I was.'

'Then she was a fool.'

His mouth twisted. 'My point exactly. Now stop arguing and wasting time, and come here. You're too far away.'

He drew her gently back into his embrace, his hands rubbing slowly up and down her arms and over her shoulders. She slipped her arms round his waist and held on, and he nuzzled her hair, making his way down until his breath sighed over her ear.

She whimpered and shifted, arching her neck to him, and his lips trailed hotly down over her jaw, following it to her chin, then down to the vulnerable hollow of her throat. She moaned softly, and he trailed back again, over her jaw, round her ear, across her eyebrow, down her nose—

Then finally, when she thought she was going to scream, his lips settled against hers with a rough sigh of satisfaction. He kissed her tenderly, nothing too demanding, nothing too hasty, and then, when she was melting against him, he lifted his head and smiled down at her. 'Better now?' he murmured.

She nodded.

'Trust me?'

She nodded again. 'Yes.'

He held her eyes for the longest moment, then his hands went to his shirt buttons, unfastened them and stripped the shirt away. The jeans followed, the shoes and socks coming off with them in one movement, until he was standing there in a pair of normal, ordinary, everyday briefs and nothing else.

She felt some of the tension go out of her. Her own

underwear was very boring and ordinary, too, but at least she now knew he didn't go in for fancy stuff.

Although what he did for his boring, ordinary briefs was definitely off the Richter scale!

'Your turn,' he prompted, and she coloured, dragging her eyes from his body and back up to his face.

He was watching her with amused tolerance, but it was laid thinly over a need that simmered barely in control. Her heart bumped in her chest, and she fumbled the hem of her T-shirt, stripping it over her head and reaching for the stud on her jeans without hesitation. The trainers were kicked aside, the jeans stripped off, and then she was standing there in her serviceable chainstore bra and pants.

She thought her legs were going to give way, but they didn't. Somehow they made it through the walk to the bed, and held her up while she flicked back the quilt. Then they deserted her, and she sat down abruptly and held out her hand to him.

He watched her, his eyes on fire. She saw his throat work, then his eyes closed. 'Molly?' he whispered.

'Yes.'

Not a question, but an answer.

He hesitated, breathing slowly, calming himself, she thought, and then he came to her...

Jack lay staring at Molly's ceiling and wondered how he'd managed to hang onto his sanity. She didn't seem to have the slightest idea how beautiful she was, how desirable. She didn't know how her vulnerability undid him, leaving him weak and shaken, desperate to hold her and protect her.

He looked down at her head, cradled against his shoulder, the soft strands of her hair teasing his jaw. He wanted to kiss her to wakefulness, slowly arousing her, waking that beautiful, wanton woman that was locked up inside her.

He wanted her again, wanted to lose himself in that generous welcome, to hold her and touch her and cherish her, to be there for her when the world fell apart and she arched sobbing in his arms.

He swallowed hard. Lord, she'd been glorious. Spectacular. He'd lost it then, well and truly, his self-control blown away by her soft cries and trembling limbs.

She stirred, lifting her head and looking up at him. 'Jack?' she murmured.

He shifted a little and kissed her. 'Hi, beautiful,' he murmured, and his voice sounded rough and unused. 'OK?'

She nodded. 'Wonderful. You?'

'Never better.'

She sighed. 'I suppose we ought to get up. I've got to pick up the children in an hour.'

'Me, too—a little before that. I tell you what, you get dressed and tidy up the bedroom, and I'll make that cup of tea—OK?'

He left her reluctantly. It was warm and inviting in the bed, lonely away from her. He pulled on his clothes, winked at her and ran down to the kitchen. It was full of her personality, sunny and bright, painted a pale cheerful yellow with a trailing vine in dark forest-green—her favourite colour—stencilled round the walls.

Busy as she was, she'd obviously found time to make it home for them all. Cassie and Philip were lucky to have her, he realised.

And so was he.

He found himself wishing she didn't have to be in a compartment, a separate part of his life, but an integral part of it instead, with him night and day, sharing all the chaos and confusion of family life.

He shook his head. It wouldn't work. It was hard enough now with only four children—and anyway, who was to say it would last? Now they'd slaked their thirst, maybe that would be the end of it.

Far from slaking his thirst, Jack realised over the next few days that the stolen time with Molly had simply whetted his appetite.

She was there in his dreams, winding through his thoughts all day, starring in his book—

It was beginning to drive him crazy. He needed her more than ever now, but there was no time. His editor was getting more and more antsy, the kids seemed to have a chaotic schedule of after-school activities, and weekends were hell.

And Seb's birthday was coming up.

'Can I have a party?' he asked, and Jack, rashly, said yes.

'Wicked! We'll have it in the barn—there's a guy with a mixing deck that does clubs and stuff. I'll find out what he charges. He's got lights and things—it'll be really cool. Oh, and can we have a sleepover?'

'In the barn?' Jack asked warily. Wicked, indeed! The thought of all those teenage boys—

'Well, the girls probably better sleep in the house, or their mums will go schizo.'

'Girls?' Jack said weakly. *Wicked?* Oh, God. 'What girls?'

Seb shrugged. 'Come on, Jack—I'm going to be fifteen. Most of my mates have got girlfriends now.'

'Have you?'

He shifted awkwardly. 'Sort of.'

Jack let out his breath in a carefully measured sigh. Talk about walking on eggshells! 'Do I know her?' he said as casually as he could manage.

'Um—you might have seen her in the shop. Her mum runs it. Her name's Al.'

'Dark hair, quite short—pretty girl?'

Seb nodded.

'OK. I take it she's coming?'

'Yeah—oh, and I've told them we'll have a barbecue— can you cook it for us? They're all going to bring something.'

Jack saw the whole weekend vanishing under the weight of this extravaganza. Still, it was more than a week away. By then, no doubt, the book would be done.

Perhaps Molly would like to come and help him host it? Maybe do some salads or something, if he paid her— perhaps a pudding.

His heart jerked in his chest, and he found himself agreeing to all sorts of things without really taking them in. He hadn't got past the fact that he might just have dreamed up a brilliant excuse to ask Molly to stay the night...

Amy had an induction day at her new senior school the next day, just before the last week of term. The school was hardly an unknown quantity, Seb had been there for two years now, but she was terribly excited. In so many ways she'd outgrown her primary school, and Jack was watching the dawning of the woman in her with increasing unease.

How would he deal with those personal issues that would have to be addressed very soon? Perhaps he could enlist Molly's help. Nick's mother would probably have something to say on the subject, but he felt her slant would be positively mediaeval and Molly might have a more relevant input.

If she'd agree.

The morning of Amy's induction day dawned hot and bright and sunny. He drove her up to the school, and there at the entrance, waving her daughter off, was Molly. His heart raced, and he parked the car on the kerb, got out and strode towards her, leaving Amy to follow.

'Molly?'

'Jack—hi! Is Amy coming here next term?'

'Yes—is Cassie?'

'Yes! I'm so glad they'll be together; they'll love it.'

They will, and I'll have a ready-made excuse to see you, he thought.

Amy ran up beside him and grinned at Molly. 'Hi, there. Is Cassie here for the induction day?'

'Yes. She's just gone in—she shouldn't be far away.'

'I'll catch her up—this is so cool!'

She waved to Jack and vanished into the crowd, weaving her way towards the door.

Jack turned to Molly, scanning her with his eyes, so pleased to see her.

'Hi,' he said, inanely, but she didn't seem to notice.

'Hi,' she said, and through her smile he thought she sounded a little breathless. She looked cool and bright and gorgeous.

'Busy?' he asked, hoping she'd say no so he could spend some time with her.

'I'm just about to do my sandwich run. What about you?'

He shrugged. 'I've dropped Nicky off at the child-minder, and Tom and Seb are at school. I ought to go and write.'

She screwed up her nose in a little smile of sympathy. 'How's it going?'

'OK,' he lied. In fact it wasn't. The hero's diminutive female client was taking too large a role, and the hero was suffering just as Jack was suffering. In a fit of meanness, Jack hadn't allowed him the privilege of intimacy with the fictional woman. In a strange way, Jack thought he might be better off that way. Intimacy with Molly had just made the whole business a lot tougher to ignore.

Which was why he found himself parking his car on the edge of the industrial estate and sitting in Molly's car, chatting to her between stops instead of writing the darned book!

She missed him. It had been lovely that morning having him with her for the sandwich run. They had hardly seen each other recently, and then only in the company of the children.

She'd see him again in a minute, too, and she'd had time to check her diary and confirm that she was free for the weekend of Seb's party.

She saw his big people-carrier pull up ahead, and he got out and walked towards her, a smile tugging at his lips. She opened the door and climbed out.

'Hi,' she said, wondering if that was really as inane as it sounded—or as breathless!

'Long time no see,' he murmured, the smile turning into a sexy grin that did silly things to her insides. 'Had a busy day?'

'Frustrating,' she said honestly, and his eyes darkened and the grin faded.

'Tell me about it,' he said in an undertone. 'So, how are you fixed for Seb's party?'

'Fine. When do you want me?'

He choked on a laugh, and she bit her lips and tried to stop the smile. 'When do you want me to come over to the house and start helping?' she rephrased.

The smile tugged at his lips. 'Whenever. The party's on Friday night, so we've got as long as possible to recover, but if you were there by six? And I don't know if you've thought about letting me hire you to do salads and puddings?'

She shook her head. 'I'll do the salads and puddings, Jack. Don't be silly. I'll make them on Friday afternoon and bring them with me.'

'Let me pay for the ingredients, at least, or I won't let you unload them from the car.'

She hesitated, but it was only sensible. She'd got to be realistic; she couldn't afford grand gestures. 'OK,' she agreed.

There was a silence then, coming out of nowhere, filled with tension. Jack sighed and scuffed his toe on the tarmac path. 'I miss you,' he said gruffly. 'There just doesn't seem to be any time together. Even this morning—you were still working, and I should have been.'

'Did you write anything this afternoon?' she asked, worried about the pressure he was under.

He sighed again. 'No. Not worth printing, anyway. I can't seem to focus.'

She chewed her lip. She was mad, but so what? 'How about if I come round this weekend and look after the kids? That way you can concentrate, and you won't have to worry about feeding them or where they are or who's keeping an eye on Nicky.'

'It's a hell of a lot to ask.'

She smiled wryly. 'I expect I'll survive—if it'll help. You might be able to make some progress then.'

She could feel the tension in him, the need to accept

warring with the need to be independent, to cope alone, to manage.

She knew all about it; she'd been there.

'Jack, it's all right to have help every now and then. Everyone needs it. It doesn't mean you've failed them.'

'You could stay,' he said, his eyes piercing, his voice gruff and unsteady.

'Yes,' she murmured. 'Yes, we could stay. I'd have to go and do the sandwiches on Sunday morning, though, but I could do them and come back.'

His lips quirked into a smile, and his eyes softened. 'Molly, you're wonderful.'

She laughed. 'You're just saying that because you want a babysitter for the weekend,' she teased.

'You guessed.' His mouth twitched again, then his eyes flared. 'Maybe we can find a moment alone together,' he murmured.

Molly laughed again. 'Don't hold your breath. With six kids around? I doubt it.'

'We can try. We should be able to snatch a few minutes to ourselves.'

She grinned. 'How does two in the morning sound?'

The kids thought it was a brilliant idea. Cassie was full of her day at her new school, and the fact that she and Amy were going to be in the same class. 'I'll be able to see her every day!' she exclaimed, delighted. Clearly they were going to have a lot to talk about over the weekend, and Philip was equally keen to get back to Tom and play in the barn again.

'Just stay away from Seb,' she warned, and he grinned.

'I will. He calls me Pipsqueak, anyway. Gross.' He shuddered, then shot off upstairs to his bedroom to pack ready for tomorrow.

'Let me have your uniform to wash now,' she called after them, and wondered if for once it would hurt if she made the sandwiches the day before and put them in the fridge.

Yes, she decided, it would matter. Damn. Why did she have to be conscientious? It just meant she'd have to get up on Sunday morning, come back, make the order for the garage and drop it off on the way back to Jack's. By the time she got there he might be awake!

Knowing she'd be busy the next morning, she put the washing on and went upstairs to pack her own bag. Her hand hovered over the condoms, then she tucked them into a pocket at the back of the case—just to be on the safe side. It was highly unlikely they'd need them, but you couldn't be too careful.

She should be safe this weekend anyway, it was a bit early in her cycle.

She packed her pretty Victorian nightie that covered her from stem to stern, because with Seb and Jack wandering about she didn't want to appear provocative or immodest.

The children were out of bed at the crack of dawn, helping to clear up after their breakfast things while she labelled the sandwiches, then they put their bags into the car, she loaded up the trays for the garage, put down plenty of food and water for the cat and they were off.

It was only one night, just a few miles away, but they were as excited as if they'd been going on holiday again. They bounced and squiggled about, sang songs and chattered endlessly, and Molly smiled to herself.

She knew exactly how they were feeling. She was excited, too, the tension building in her so that by the time they arrived her heart was pounding, her palms were prickling and she was sure her cheeks must have a hectic flush.

Jack was outside, pottering in the garden with Nicky and the dog, and he came over to her car with one of those lovely crinkly smiles around his eyes. He opened the door and helped her out, his hands lingering on hers just a moment longer than was necessary.

'Hi,' he murmured. 'All done?'

She nodded. 'Yes. I'm all yours.'

He gave a hollow laugh.

'I wish,' he said under his breath. 'God, I wish.'

Then he hugged her, reached for her bag and shut the door. 'Come on in, I'll show you to your room.'

The kids had run in with Amy and Tom, and she followed him up the stairs and down the landing. 'This is the spare room,' he said, pushing the door open and ushering her in.

'Oh, it's lovely,' she exclaimed, looking round at the pretty furnishings.

He pushed the door shut with his foot. 'You look gorgeous. Come here, I need to kiss you.'

She took a step towards him and the door flew open. 'Is Molly sleeping in here?' Amy asked.

'Yes,' Jack said, rolling his eyes at Molly. 'Why?'

'Just wondered. That's fine—she's near us.'

'All the better to keep tabs on you, young ladies,' she said with a dredged-up smile, and wondered how rational she was to feel such enormous disappointment because they'd been interrupted before that kiss...

CHAPTER SEVEN

'COFFEE?' Jack offered, when it was obvious they weren't going to get a minute's peace.

'Lovely—and then you must go and get on,' she told him firmly.

His mouth quirked. 'Are you nagging me?'

'Absolutely. I'm here to help you, not to distract you or provide you with a displacement activity.'

He chuckled. 'Sounds interesting,' he murmured, softly so that the children didn't hear.

'In your dreams,' she murmured back, and went downstairs to the relative safety of the kitchen. The children seemed to erupt into it, as they erupted everywhere, and Jack dished out juice and breakfast cereal while the kettle boiled.

'We're a little on the drag,' he confessed, warming the coffee pot. 'We don't get up as early as you—well, they don't, anyway.' He nodded his head towards the older three, sitting down at the table and piling into their breakfast. 'Nicky and I have been up for ages, haven't we, sweetheart?'

'And Boy,' Nicky said firmly.

'And Boy, but we woke him up when we came down. Who wants tea?'

Molly sat on the sofa and watched him dealing with the clamouring hordes. It was like a nest of baby birds, she thought, all squawking furiously, beaks open.

And hers were joining in, even though they'd already had breakfast. Within minutes the kitchen was a scene of total devastation, and then he handed her a mug of coffee, jerked his head in the direction of the door and led her into the relative peace and tranquillity of the study.

The door closed behind them with a defiant click.

'It's like an oasis,' she said with a laugh as the quiet settled around them.

He grimaced. 'Sometimes. Sometimes it feels like a prison.' He put his coffee down, took hers from her and drew her into his arms.

'They'll come in,' she warned.

He grinned and leant on the door. 'Only if they push us over first. Now, about that kiss.'

His lips were warm and coaxing, and after a moment she relaxed against him and just enjoyed it. It was wonderful to be held by him, to feel the thud of his heart against hers, the warmth of his arms, the gentle pressure of his kiss.

'Open your mouth,' he murmured, just as the door lurched behind him and he released her. 'Hang on, I've dropped something,' he lied, and, handing her a mug, he pushed her towards the other side of the desk.

She sat down, hands cradling the mug, and he picked up the other one and opened the door.

'Yes, Seb?'

'Can I go round to Al's?' he asked, his voice shifting octaves again as it often did when he was uptight about something—or trying not to laugh.

'If you're back by twelve-thirty—and don't go out of the village.'

'OK. We're probably just going to lie around in her room and play music, anyway.' He paused, staring at the mug, then flicked his eyes up to Jack's. 'When did you start taking milk in your coffee?' he asked with the ghost of a smile, and Molly buried her nose in the mug and tried not to laugh.

Jack shut the door behind him and frowned. 'I think he might be on to us,' he murmured.

'I'd say so. Whoops.' She smiled, but Jack looked worried still. 'Does it matter?' she asked softly.

'I don't know. That depends on what he thinks is going on and how he feels about it. I certainly don't want the others to know.'

She stood up, swapping mugs, and headed for the door.

'In which case,' she said logically, 'it would be sensible not to try and sneak off and make out in the corners.'

'I don't feel sensible,' he muttered.

'I noticed.'

She shut the door behind her, went back into the kitchen and set about the clearing up.

'Molly, can we go shopping?'

Amy perched herself on the arm of the sofa and watched her as she wiped the table. Cassie was sprawled on the sofa, cuddling the dog.

Molly paused, shooting Amy a curious glance. 'Shopping for what, my love?'

Amy looked embarrassed. 'Just—girl stuff. I think I need a bra.'

'Ah.' Molly swiped the last crumbs off the table, rinsed out the cloth and sat down. 'Well, could you wait a week or two? Cassie probably needs one soon as well, so we could take a day out when Jack's finished his book and go to town together—maybe have lunch and do all the girly things?'

They nodded, Cassie now hanging over the back of the sofa and watching her. 'Can we go to the shopping mall?'

Molly's heart sank. 'Maybe,' she said, hedging her bets.

She hated the drive to the big shopping centre, and her feet always ached before she'd got out of the car, just with the thought.

'I expect Jack could take us, and we could split up,' Amy offered. 'He could take Nicky and the boys, and we could go with you.'

'We'll see,' she said, trotting out the other standby. 'But anyway, we aren't going anywhere like that until he's finished the book.'

Cassie bounded off the sofa and came over to her. 'Can we make a cake?'

'Sure. Where's Nicky?'

'With the boys. They're outside in the garden, and she's in the sandpit. She's fine.'

Molly went outside and checked, just to be sure. Nicky was quite happy, and so were the boys, but Molly told them to bring her in if she became difficult or if they wanted to do something elsewhere. She left the front door propped open so she could see from the kitchen into the garden, and then she and the girls set about making a cake.

It was a chocolate cake, by popular request, and amazingly Jack had all the ingredients. 'We make cakes sometimes,' Amy told her. 'He puts on Mummy's apron and pretends to be a girl.'

Molly's mouth almost dropped. Jack, in an apron, pretending to be a girl? This she had to see!

'So, can he cook, then?'

Amy screwed up her nose a bit. 'Sort of. Not like my Mum.'

Oh, dear. 'Well, in a few minutes we can take him a piece of cake and another coffee—'

'Do I smell cake?'

She turned and looked over her shoulder at him. 'You do. You must have radar.'

He chuckled and came and loomed over her, sniffing appreciatively at the oven. 'Looks good,' he murmured. 'How did you know chocolate cake's my favourite?'

'Because it's everybody's favourite?' she offered drily.

He laughed and straightened up. 'Probably. I could kill a coffee.'

'How's it going?'

He nodded slowly. 'Better. It's coming on. I've finally stopped editing it to death and I'm moving on now.'

He was very close still, and she reached up and tweaked his nose affectionately. 'Good. Why don't you go in the garden for ten minutes, check on the boys and Nicky, and I'll bring you out a coffee in the fresh air?'

'Good idea.'

He hesitated, and for one crazy second she thought he was going to kiss her, but he seemed to recover his senses—either that or she'd misunderstood him completely. He moved away, and the breath seemed to shift again in her lungs.

Crazy. Not even Jack would be that mad.

'Hi.'

She looked up from the kettle and smiled sleepily. 'Hi. I hope I didn't wake you.'

He shook his head. 'No. I was awake—I wondered when you'd be getting up.'

'I have to go to work,' she reminded him.

'I know. Is that tea you're making?'

'Yes—unless you want coffee?'

He dropped into the sofa, stretching out his long bare legs from under the hem of the towelling robe and fondling the dog's ears. 'No, tea's great. Thanks.'

She dragged her eyes from his legs. 'What time do the others wake up?'

'Oh, whenever. Nicky's usually first, then the other two, then Seb. Why?'

She smiled. 'Just wondering who was going to interrupt us this time if I try and kiss you good morning.'

He chuckled and held out his arms. 'No one. Come here.'

'There's the small matter of the dog in the way.'

'No, he's not. Sit on my lap and we'll talk about the first thing that comes up.'

Her eyes widened. 'Mr Haddon!' she exclaimed softly. 'The very idea!'

He gave a lopsided grin and shrugged. 'It was worth a try. I still want a kiss.'

She went to the back door, opened it and shut the dog out for a moment. 'Right. Where were we?'

He patted the sofa and she sat down on the warm place left by Boy, leant into his arms and kissed him.

'Mmm,' he murmured against her lips, and his warm, firm hand cupped her breast through her old-fashioned nightdress. 'This is like a tantalising chastity belt,' he said laughingly, but then the laughter died, his head came down on hers again and their lips melded in a wild and desperate kiss that left them both aching for more.

'This is hell,' he groaned, burying his head in her shoulder. 'I need you, Molly. It seems such a long time.'

'Just over a week—ten days.'

'It feels like ten years.'

'Just finish your book and we can snatch some time.'

He gave a hollow laugh. 'When? The kids are on holiday from next Thursday, for six weeks. *Six weeks*, Molly!'

'They go to Holiday Club sometimes.'

'Seb doesn't.'

'But Seb doesn't need a babysitter.'

'No, but Nicky does, and I probably won't have finished the book.'

She sat up, pushing him away, and looked into his weary eyes. 'When does it have to be done?'

'ASAP. The final draft needs to go off to production in October, but there's a lot to do between now and then—tweaking and fiddling.'

'So go and tweak and fiddle. You're up now—make a start. I'll be back in a couple of hours. Let's just have this tea and we can both get on.'

She stood up, let the dog in, poured the tea and sat at the other end of the sofa, with Boy curled up between them trying hopelessly to be small. 'You,' she told the dog, 'are a nuisance.'

Jack laughed softly. 'Another inheritance—and the cat. They were all part of the same package.'

And Jack, being the softie he was, had taken them all in and made them welcome.

Now, why didn't that surprise her?

'How are you doing?'

Jack stretched and looked round the kitchen. Molly was at the table helping Nicky with something messy and indeterminate—a pasta picture?—Tom and Philip were outside in the garden with the dog, he could hear Amy and Cassie overhead, and somewhere in the distance was the hideous pounding of Seb's music system.

'OK,' he replied. 'I thought I'd take a break. I've been at it since six—I need to stand back a little from it.' He went to the fridge and pulled out a carton of juice, pouring himself a hefty slug. 'Oh, that's good. I've had too much coffee.'

'Your choice,' she reminded him.

He grinned. 'I'm working on being sterile—don't want any accidents, do we?'

He ruffled Nicky's hair affectionately, and she flashed him a grin and carried on sticking, her tongue wedged in the corner of her mouth just like Amy when she was concentrating.

He pulled out a chair and sat opposite them, watching Molly with hungry eyes. They absorbed every detail of her—the soft curl of her hair, the way her lashes swept down over her cheeks when she was bending over Nicky, the quick, ready smile for him when she glanced up—it was heaven and hell rolled into one, and he wouldn't be anywhere else in the world.

He was falling in love with her, he realised. How foolish. It would never work, not with six children to cope with. Four, maybe, two each, but six?

What if it went wrong? They'd had enough heartache and disruption in their lives, without losing Molly, and her children had lost their father when he walked away. How would they cope if it happened again?

Apart from which, just the thought of all those children was enough to make his hair stand on end.

He managed to ignore the fact that he'd got more done in the last twenty-four hours than he had in the last two weeks. That was coincidence, just the stage he was at in the book, when things began to flow and take over and the words seemed to write themselves.

Nothing to do with Molly's presence, taking pressure off him and warming him with her sunny personality and her beautiful smile—

'How about a picnic lunch, if you want to get away from the book for a while?'

He looked up, startled, and met Molly's eyes. 'What?'

'I said—'

'I heard you. We haven't got anything to eat.'

'Oh, we have—if you can cope with my sandwiches again.'

A picnic. Lord, he hadn't had a picnic for years!

'Sounds good,' he agreed. 'There should be a couple of cartons of juice and some chocolate biscuits and crisps and things.'

'And fruit, and yoghurts.'

'Where shall we go?'

'Don't know. How about Sutton Heath? The dog can have a good run there, as well. We could all go for a walk, in fact—do us good. Do you good. It might get your blood circulating a little and shift some of the slurry off your brain.'

He snorted. It sounded like an excellent idea! 'Great. Let's go. I'll get the kids organised, you clean Nicky up.'

'Nicky doing picture,' the child protested.

'But it needs time to dry now before you can do any more, or the paper will be too soggy,' Molly reasoned, and Jack stuck his head out of the front door, suppressing a grin.

'How about a picnic, boys?'

'Yeah—where?'

'Molly suggested Sutton Heath.'

'Oh, yeah! We can play in the woods.'

'Get ready, then, and wash your hands.' He ran upstairs, told the girls, and thumped on Seb's door.

It opened and he stood there, bleary-eyed. No doubt he'd been watching videos until two again. 'We're going for a picnic,' Jack said.

'That's nice. Have fun.'

'No—you're coming.'

'Why—so I can babysit Nicky while you and Molly sneak off and hold hands?'

Jack hung onto his temper with difficulty. 'No. So you can get a little fresh air into your lungs and absorb a little natural beauty instead of lying here listening to that trash and watching violent movies all night.'

'I wasn't—'

'Seb, I heard the television on in your room at after midnight. Don't argue with me, please. Just get ready and come.'

The door banged shut in Jack's face, and he shook his head, went into his room and grabbed a sweater, just in case it was chilly there near the sea. The weather had been a bit hit and miss, and although it seemed nice enough now, he knew it might change. He found sweatshirts for all the children, ran downstairs and met Molly in the kitchen doorway with the coolbox in her arms.

'Here.'

He took it and filed it in the car, then the kids and Boy piled in.

'What about Seb?'

'I'm here,' he said grumpily from behind them.

'Right. Let's go.'

Seb went to the front door of the car, but Jack stopped him. 'Molly's going there. Can you sit in the back with the boys, please?'

He met Seb's defiant glare over the top of the car, and for a moment he wondered if he was going to have a fight on his hands. Then Seb gave a short sigh, opened the side door and got in behind Molly's seat, slamming the door shut with unnecessary force.

Jack got in, started the engine and glanced across at Molly. She was looking worried, and he shot her an encouraging smile. Damn Seb, he thought, and then stifled the thought. Seb had been there first, Seb always travelled in the front of the car, Seb was his responsibility.

Molly, bless her dear, sweet heart, was just a diversion.

The thought saddened him immeasurably.

'Any more?'

Tom peered hopefully into the bottom of the coolbox. 'An apple,' he said, disgusted.

'You've had tons,' Molly said with a laugh, and he screwed up his face and sighed.

'OK,' he said heavily. 'I don't suppose I'll starve to death.'

'No, I don't suppose you will.'

'Come on, let's all go for a walk,' Jack said decisively, getting to his feet. 'We'll pack this lot away and take Boy for a run, then we'll go on down to Bawdsey and buy an ice-cream.'

'Yeah!'

The boys jumped up, zooming off into the woods with arms outstretched, playing aeroplanes. The girls packed up the picnic stuff with Molly, and Jack took Nicky into some bushes for the inevitable call of nature.

Molly looked across at Seb, sitting a little way apart, munching disconsolately on an apple. He seemed miserable for some reason.

She went over to him. 'Seb?'

He didn't look up. 'What?' he muttered.

'I'm sorry if you felt I took your place in the car.'

He shrugged. 'That's OK.'

'Coming for a walk with us?' she asked, sitting down beside him.

'Why? You don't want me.'

'Seb, that's not true—'

'It is. Jack certainly doesn't. He gets at me the whole time.'

Oh, dear. She groped carefully for the right words, and decided she didn't know them. She'd just have to tell him what she felt. 'He's just trying to do the best for you, Seb,' she began. 'It can't be easy, taking on someone else's children, no matter how well you think you know them. He worries about you a lot, and he does love you; I know that.'

Seb snorted and hurled the apple core into the under-growth. 'No, he doesn't. He tolerates me. He loves the others—especially Nicky. You'd think Nicky was his, the way he carries on.'

'Nicky *is* his—at least, as much as any of you are. He's cared for her from birth, so of course they're close, but he'll fight with her when she's a teenager, just as he does with you. It won't be any different.'

'Oh, yeah?'

'Yes. Trust me, teenagers and parents always fight—unless the parents just give in the whole time, and that doesn't help anyone.'

'You sound just like Jack.'

She smiled gently. 'If you don't mind, I'll take that as a compliment.' She stood up, brushing off her jeans. 'Come with us, Seb—please?'

He sighed, but he got to his feet and followed her when she went to join the others.

She fell in beside Jack, and he shot her a curious look. 'What was that about?'

'Parenting. I think he's jealous of your relationship with Nicky.'

'Hardly,' he said with a dry chuckle. 'I can't see Seb on my knee watching television.'

'Do you ever hug him?'

Jack looked at her in amazement. 'Hug him? He'd kill me.'

'I don't think so. I don't want to interfere, but I just wonder if he misses the hugs and cuddles of childhood, and because you aren't his father, he feels he can't just walk up to you and hug you like he would have done with Nick or Jan.'

He sighed heavily. 'What the hell can I do about that?'

'Well, you could hug him.'

'He'd think I was mad!'

'No, he wouldn't. Just a quick hug in passing. Trust me, Jack. I think he needs it. He's feeling very lonely and isolated. You've got me, Amy and Tom have got Cassie and Philip, Nicky's got everybody—'

'And Seb's all alone. Hell. I hadn't looked at it like that.'

They went on a little further, and she glanced over her shoulder to check the children. Nicky was walking with the girls, swinging from their hands, the boys were still rushing about being planes, and Seb was trailing them, kicking stones and looking bored.

'I'm going to walk with the boys, show them bugs and things,' she told Jack. 'Why don't you find yourself next to Seb?'

'He'll smell a rat.'

'No, he won't. Look, the dog's down a rabbit hole right beside him. Go and sort the dog out, throw him a stick and you'll be right there with Seb.'

Would it work? Goodness knows. It couldn't make it worse, she didn't suppose. She intercepted the boys in mid-flight. 'Hey, you two, why don't you stop screaming around and being fighter jets, and come and see what we can find in here?'

She led them off the track, found a rotten log and carefully lifted the bark. Hundreds of little woodlice and other insects ran about in a frenzy, and the boys squatted down and watched them, fascinated.

'Wow, they're really funny,' Tom said with a laugh. He picked one up and it curled into a tight ball. 'I'm going to put it down Amy's neck,' he said, but Molly grabbed him by the seat of his jeans just as he turned to run off, and pulled him back.

'No,' she said firmly. 'It'll get hurt. Put it back.'

'Oooohh,' he protested, but she was adamant, and so the poor little thing was returned to its home.

'Come on, let's see what else we can find—oh, look, up there! See the hole in the side of that old tree? It must be a house for someone—a woodpecker, maybe, or a squirrel.'

'There's a squirrel,' Philip said softly, pointing to a nearby tree. The little fellow bounced around, then scooted up the trunk and vanished in the treetops.

'See what else you can spot,' she encouraged, and then left them to it. The girls were getting bored with swinging Nicky, and she went towards them, watching Jack and Seb out of the corner of her eye. They were walking side by side, not talking, but Seb had lost his rebellious look and Jack looked relaxed.

Good. It was a start, at least.

'Hi, girls,' she said cheerfully.

'Hi, Molly.'

'Hi, Mum. Mum, Nicky's being a pain.'

'Surely not,' she said with a smile. 'Nicky, hold my hand, darling.'

Nicky tucked her hand inside her armpit and turned away. 'No. Want Amy an' Cassie.'

'All right, stay with Amy and Cassie, but they're tired, darling. They can't carry you. You'll have to walk.'

'Jack carry,' she said, and, turning round, she ran towards him, her chubby little legs going like pistons.

She arrived between Seb and Jack, held up both hands and grinned disarmingly. 'Swing me,' she demanded.

Seb and Jack exchanged a resigned smile, took the little hands and swung her. Behind her, Molly could hear them, 'One, two, three, *swing*!' over and over again.

Well, she thought, at least they were working together now. Good old Nicky.

The girls were chatting, the boys had vanished, their presence given away by crashing noises in the undergrowth, and the others were involved with their swinging.

'Here, Boy,' she said, turning to the dog. 'Come and keep me company.'

He ran up beside her, tail wagging, and dropped a disgusting, spitty stick at her feet.

'Oh, yum, love. You want me to touch that?'

He grinned, tongue lolling, and she picked it up and hurled it as far as she could.

It wasn't far enough. Within seconds he was back, grinning at her again, ready for another throw.

Oh, well. There was nothing else to do and it had been her idea.

She turned round towards Jack, now strolling along with Nicky on his shoulders, and he winked at her.

She smiled back, ridiculously warmed by the gesture, and picked up the disgusting stick again...

The weekend seemed light-years away, and Jack missed Molly more than ever. Still, he'd made huge progress with his book, and he was in the swing now. He wrote while Nicky was at the childminder's, thought and planned and dreamed the book the rest of the day and night, and for the first time he began to believe he'd finish it before his editor passed him on to another publishing house in disgust!

Then Seb's party loomed in the way, a total distraction just when he didn't need it, and he had to take time out to go shopping for the food and for a present.

Seb wanted a colour television for his bedroom, but Jack's gut instinct was to take away the old black and white one that was in there to stop him watching rubbish all night, so he certainly didn't feel inclined to make it *more* inviting!

Anyway, it was hardly high on Jack's list of priorities for spending. He decided in the end to buy him a new computer, because he'd need it more than ever with his GCSEs and A levels coming up, and the old one in the snug was stretched to the limit as it was.

Then one evening, after Al had come round to help Seb get ready for the party, he went into the barn to see how they were doing and caught them looking guilty and embarrassed. They were standing miles apart, both flushed, eyes bright, and Jack felt his heart sink.

Not sex, he thought. Not already. He's only fifteen on Saturday!

'How are you doing?' he asked with forced cheer. 'Worked out where the lights are going?'

Seb cleared his throat. 'Yeah—sort of. We thought we'd ask you. We can't decide.'

Or haven't given it a moment's thought. Jack remembered the conversation about going round to Al's and lying around in her room listening to music. *Lying around?* he thought. *In her bedroom? On her bed?* Oh, Lord.

They sorted out the positioning of the lights, he vetoed dragging spare mattresses down from the attic and spreading them around for people to sit on, and suggested instead that they find the old rugs from the attic and lay them on the floor.

'You can bring over all the cushions from the snug and the kitchen, and the bean bags, and some pillows, if you like, but not mattresses.'

'Why not?' Seb argued.

'Because I wasn't born yesterday,' Jack told him softly, 'and you guys don't need any encouragement.'

Seb had the grace to blush. 'OK. We'll get the rugs.'

It wasn't finished, Jack thought. He'd have to have another talk with him.

Later that night, the night before the party, he knocked on Seb's door. The kids were all in bed and Seb was watching television. He came to the door. 'Yeah?'

The cloying scent of incense sticks hit him like a wall. 'Can I come in?'

Seb looked wary, but he opened the door. It was chaos. He threw some clothes off the armchair onto the floor, and turned the television down. 'What do you want?' he asked, getting straight to the point.

Jack sat down in the chair and wondered if he'd get through this conversation without doing more harm than good.

'It's about Al—you and Al.'

Seb dropped onto the bed, crossed his legs and leant back against the wall, trying to look nonchalant. 'What about us?'

'Seb, I'm not a child—'

'Nor am I.'

'I know.'

Seb blinked. Jack ignored him and carried on. 'I just—it's very easy, when you're young and things get out of hand, to imagine that nothing can go wrong.'

'Nothing's going to get out of hand. I just kissed her, Jack! For God's sake, chill!'

'No, I won't chill. I'm not saying you can't kiss her. I'm just saying that—feelings get out of control very easily. Your hormones are all over the place at the moment, and so are hers.' So are mine, he thought, heaven help me. 'I just wanted to say, whatever happens, you need to be able to wake up in the morning and look at yourself in the mirror. Don't hurt her, Seb—or yourself. Treat yourselves with respect. Be careful. Be sensible. Don't put yourself in a situation where it's too easy for things to get out of control.'

He stood up, slid his hand into his pocket and dropped something on the bed.

Seb's eyes widened.

'Just in case,' Jack said. 'It's not an invitation to be stupid. It's a safety net. Use wisely—preferably not at all.'

And he walked out, taking with him an image of Seb, scarlet-cheeked and wide-eyed, staring at the packet of condoms.

CHAPTER EIGHT

'WHERE can I hide this?'

Jack looked up from the barbecue and straightened slowly. 'You've made him a birthday cake.'

'Yes—why, have you got one?'

He shook his head. 'I haven't had a minute. I was going to make one, but nothing like that.'

'We need to hide it till tomorrow.'

'Yes—in the filing cabinet in my study. He'll never look in there. Molly, you're a brick.'

'Hmm.' She smiled at him. 'I've never been sure I wanted to be something hard and square.'

'Don't worry, you're a soft, curvy brick.'

'Thanks.'

She gave a wry grin and followed him into the study. 'In there?'

He opened the drawer, and closed it with the cake safely installed. 'I'll even lock it, just to be on the safe side.'

He dropped the key into his desk drawer, shuffled some papers onto it and went back to the garden. The barbecue was set up outside the door, and he was lighting it now to get it just right for eight.

'My brother's got a gas one,' Molly said, watching him pile the coals up and drench them in lighting fluid.

'Sounds like a good idea,' he growled, dropping the second match. 'I'm frying my fingers here.'

'Turn the knob, press the ignition button—'

131

'All right, all right!' He got it going at last and straightened up with a sigh. 'Right. Salads and puds all inside?'

'For now.'

'Amy and Cassie are pinning paper onto the wallpapering table so we can put the food on it. I thought if we put it outside the kitchen window, we could pass the stuff out. It also keeps it a little way away from the barbecue so they won't get burned.'

'Sounds good. Got time for a cup of tea?'

'No—but I've got time for a glass of wine. Join me?'

She laughed. 'It'll be fine, Jack.'

'If the girls don't all get pregnant. I had a chat to Seb, by the way. Remind me to tell you about it.'

Her curiosity was well and truly piqued, but she didn't follow up on it because the children were milling around it and it didn't seem like the time.

The DJ arrived and set up his gear, and as one the local wildlife shot under cover and clapped its paws over its ears.

'Do you suppose it's loud enough?' Molly yelled at Jack.

He rolled his eyes, went into the barn and a moment later the volume was halved. He came out again grinning.

'How did you manage that? They're normally extraordinarily resistant to turning it down.'

The grin widened. 'I told him the barn would fall down because the vibrations would damage the already fragile structure. I don't think he wanted to die.'

'You are joking,' Molly said, worried.

He chuckled. 'Of course I'm joking. The barn's as sound as a bell. I wouldn't let the kids in there if it wasn't.'

'What about upstairs?'

'It's fine. I've replaced the loose and rotten boards. Relax.'

'I'm relaxed,' she said with a smile. 'What can I do? Where's Nicky?'

'With the girls, I think, upstairs. Would you like to make sure they don't put on too much make-up? Seb has said they can join them for the barbecue and perhaps a dance, but they've got to come out of the barn by nine, and I don't want Nicky within a hundred miles of it.'

'What about the boys?'

'What about them? They'll just hang around and eat.'

She laughed and went upstairs to see what was going on. The girls were dressed in jeans and pretty tops, the boys were in their usual jeans and sweatshirts and trainers, and Nicky had a jumpsuit on with a sweatshirt under it.

'You look nice,' Amy said, admiring the floaty crinkle-cotton dress Molly was wearing.

'Thank you, darling. I expect I'll freeze but never mind.'

There was a bit of commotion on the drive, and Molly leant over and peered through the window. 'Everyone's arriving,' she told them.

They whooped and charged for the stairs, Nicky toddling in their wake. Molly took her hand, smiled at her and went down with a little more dignity.

Jack glanced up and saw Molly coming down the stairs, Nicky's hand in hers, and his heart thudded against his ribs. She looked gorgeous. The breeze was channelled up the stairs, making her skirt drift against her legs, and he closed his eyes and counted to ten.

Now was not the time!

*   *   *

'It seems to be going well.'

Jack looked down at Molly in surprise. She'd crept up on him while he was tending the last remnants of the barbecue, and he hadn't heard her coming. Not surprising, really. The volume had sneaked up again, and he could hardly hear himself think.

'Mmm,' he agreed. 'It's a good job we haven't got neighbours too close.'

She chuckled and reached out, picking up a chipolata in her fingers. 'Yum,' she mumbled, biting into it and chewing hungrily. 'I sort of missed supper.'

'Get a plate—in fact, get two. I think they've all finished eating now. We'll tackle the leftovers.'

They piled their plates with odd things—lettuce obviously wasn't popular, although the cherry tomatoes had gone, and the pasta salad was almost finished although some of the rice was still there. Still, they managed to find enough bits and pieces, and sat down on the bench under the apple tree and ate hungrily.

'Kids all in bed?' Jack asked her round a forkful of chicken.

'Yup—although I doubt if they're asleep. It's a good job Nicky sleeps at the back.'

'She'd sleep standing up on the drive she's so tired,' he said drily, and bit into a shrivelled sausage. 'I'll go and check them in a minute. Got any puds left?'

She smiled. 'I saved you some chocolate mousse cake.'

His eyes flared and he grinned. 'You are the best,' he said with feeling, and, putting his plate down, he went inside to check the children.

A few minutes later he came out juggling two bowls of chocolate cake, a couple of glasses hooked over one finger and a bottle of wine.

'Dessert, madam,' he murmured.

She took the bowls from him and swapped one for a glass of wine. 'Mmm, lovely,' she sighed, sipping it. 'It's like sherry, almost. It's gorgeous. What is it?'

'It's a dessert wine—about fifteen per cent proof. It'll knock your socks off.'

'I'm not wearing socks.'

'You're not, are you? Are you warm enough?'

She nodded. She was snuggled into a cosy lambswool cardigan, and she was fine. Well, her feet were a bit chilly, but she'd live.

She turned sideways on the bench, tucked her feet under his lean, warm thigh and sighed. 'Now I'm warm enough,' she said, and savoured the chocolate mousse cake. It was gorgeous, as always, a foolproof recipe that was her standby. 'Yum. This is really nice, with the kids tucked up and the others all busy enjoying themselves.'

'Except for the ones that keep sneaking out for a cigarette.'

'Are there many?' she asked.

'Enough. They can't see me here. I've been watching them, off and on. They think they're so cool.'

'Is Seb there?'

'No.' He gave a sigh. 'No, I expect he's inside making out with Alison. I had a chat with him.'

'What about?'

'Sex—contraception—self-respect.'

'My God.' Molly took a sip of wine and watched him in the moonlight. 'That must have been an interesting conversation.'

'I don't know about that. He didn't say a lot. I gave him my condoms, as we don't seem to be about to use them.'

She laughed softly. 'I wonder what their shelf-life is? I expect they'll perish before we get a chance.'

His hand came down and cupped her cold ankles, hard and warm and possessive. 'One day,' he sighed. His hand slid up her skirt, brushing the soft fabric aside, and came to rest on her thigh, fingers curled loosely over the top, caressing her lightly. 'You feel so good,' he murmured. 'Such soft skin—tender and delicate. I could just bite it.'

She chuckled. 'Have some more cake instead.'

Jack laughed and hugged her, turning her so she was curled against his side. The kids were quiet, the barn seemed to be heaving happily, and in the deep shadow of the old tree he bent his head and kissed her.

Heat poured through her, making her whimper with need, and he cradled her jaw and rested his head against hers. 'Don't,' he groaned softly. He nibbled his way down her jaw, over the hollow of her throat, over the fine arch of her collarbone, pushing the dress aside so he could lay a trail of hot, open-mouthed kisses across the soft swell of her breasts.

'Jack!' she gasped under her breath. His hand snaked up her skirt again, coming to rest against the warm curve of her hip. His fingers hooked under the elastic of her knickers and flicked it teasingly, and then with a sigh of satisfaction he slid his hand round and cupped her with his palm.

'This is cruel,' she whispered, arching into his hand.

'Tell me about it.' His hand moved slowly, then with a muffled curse he removed it, slipped her dress down over her legs again and straightened up.

'What?'

'The kids are sneaking out again,' he murmured under

his breath. 'I'm just going to go and make sure there are no drugs or anything like that. You stay here.'

As if she could go anywhere! Her legs were like jelly, her mind was scrambled and it had nothing whatever to do with the wine!

'Damn you, Jack Haddon,' she murmured to herself. 'You're driving me crazy!'

She picked up the wine bottle, tipped a little more into her glass and sipped it. If she was going to be squiffy and legless, she might as well have a good reason!

Seb's party was declared a huge success. His friends left by midnight, Jack and Molly settled the few that were staying on cushions in the barn, and by two it was quiet. Molly had gone to bed, and Jack did a last quiet recce round the garden before going to bed himself.

He slept with his window open, so that he could hear any noise from the barn, and it was after ten the next morning before they emerged, a little tired but otherwise unharmed.

There had been no drugs, only a few had been smoking and there had hardly been any alcohol, just the odd can of beer. All in all, Jack thought, they'd got away with it quite lightly.

And, once the last friends had gone home, they gave Seb his birthday presents.

'It's a telly!' he said, unwrapping the box.

'Er—not exactly,' Jack warned him, but then as the paper came off the boy's eyes widened. 'Wow—my own computer! Oh, wicked, Jack, thanks!'

For a moment he thought Seb was going to get up and hug him, but he subsided again with a huge sigh and an even bigger grin. 'Oh, that is just excellent! Thanks, Jack. Thanks a lot.'

Jack smiled, a little awkward and touched by his obvious delight, and then he caught Molly's eye. She was looking pleased, smiling warmly at him. Bless her, she was such a star.

'Open the others,' he prompted.

Amy had given him a book, Tom had given him a set of pens and Nicky had chosen chocolate bunnies in a box.

'You'll have to help me eat them,' he said to her, and she held out her hand for the first one.

'Later, maybe,' Jack suggested, and then Molly handed him a small, flat package.

'It's not much—just something from the three of us.'

It was a computer game, an inter-active empire-building game of strategy which Jack had advised her he might want. It seems he'd hit the button. 'Excellent! Oh, wow, it's just what I wanted. That's great, thanks!'

And to Jack's astonishment, he got up and kissed her cheek. 'You're a cool dude, Molly,' he said with a grin, then swaggered over to the kettle. 'Anyone for tea?'

The house was quiet. The children were all in bed, even Seb had gone up to his room and was playing on his computer having demolished his birthday cake with a little help. Molly was curled up in the snug with a book, and Jack was just burning up the keys trying to get down a scene that was eating him alive.

Toby, the PI, was about to be shut in a safe, and Maddy was going to set him free. Jack, playing God, had decided she was an amateur safe-breaker and mini-sleuth in her own right, and he was on the edge of his seat until he'd committed it to the computer.

Sweat stood out on his brow, his palms were clammy with fear, and the soles of his feet were prickling.

Stay calm, Toby told himself. Don't panic. Breathe nice and slowly, move as little as possible. Cut down your demand for air. Oh, God. Fear rose like bile in his throat—

Jack swallowed hard and consciously steadied his thrashing heart. 'It's just a book,' he muttered.

Time seemed to go in a blur. He thought he'd passed out at one point, but something woke him. A scratching noise, clicking—a little clunk. More clicking and clunking.

Rats?

Or someone opening the safe?

'Toby?'

'Maddy?' he croaked. *His eyes were screwed up against the light, and he felt her hands reach in and drag him out into the clean, sweet air. Tears scalded his eyes and he reached for her, clinging to her, hanging on while he got his breath back.*

'I thought I'd got away from you,' he rasped.

'Nah, you don't get that lucky. You're stuck with me, Toby,' she whispered, *her throat clogged with emotion. He squeezed her tight. There were no words.*

'You need to sleep,' she told him.

He didn't remember the journey afterwards, just waking up in her bed, her soft warmth against his side, the gentle puff of her breath against his cheek.

He watched her, and after a moment she opened her eyes.

'Hi,' she whispered.

'Hi.'

'You OK?'

He nodded.

Her hands reached for him, trailing over his chest. 'Good, because I've got plans for you—'

Jack closed his eyes and gave a shaky sigh. This was it. He couldn't hold them back any longer. He stopped thinking and just let his fingers feel the words, let them flow.

Her body was soft and yet hard, sleek muscle and feminine curve combining to unman him.

'Come,' she whispered.

His heart pounded, his body ached with frustration, aroused to the point of pain by the wild and tempestuous scene he created.

It was all right for them, their lovemaking came to a natural conclusion, he thought in frustration. Unlike his—

'I love you, Maddy,' he mouthed. She shifted against him, slaked for now, and he lay there and thought how he might have died and never known this joy.

His hands curled protectively round her, and Toby closed his eyes and gave himself up to sleep…

'Molly?'

She was sleeping, her head at an awkward angle, the book abandoned in her lap. He brushed the hair gently off her face and kissed her, and she woke with a start.

'Jack?' she whispered.

'Who else?'

'What time is it?'

He looked at his watch. 'Two-thirty.'

'I must have gone to sleep. Sorry. I meant to stay up to keep you company.'

'Don't worry.' He drew her to her feet. 'Come for a walk.' He needed activity. After that scene, with all its attendant emotions, he needed to move, to walk outside in the fresh air, to talk to Molly.

To hold her.

He swallowed. He wanted her, needed her. The kids were all asleep.

She stood up, slipping her feet into her shoes and following him out into the cool, soft night. The clouds were chasing across the moon, shadows racing over the fields, the light bright as day at times, dim at others.

He drew her into his arms, and she slipped hers around him and snuggled close, then hesitated, feeling his arousal.

'Jack?' she whispered.

He found her mouth, soft and sweet and tempting, and a shudder ran through him. She gave a little sigh and rose up on tiptoe, pressing herself to him, sliding against him in the sweetest torture.

'Molly, I need you,' he said, his voice low and ragged.

She kissed him, her tongue tormenting him, playing with fire.

He took her hand, leading her into the barn. They'd be safe there; the kids were fast asleep. Even Seb's room had been quiet as they'd come past the bottom of the stairs.

No one would disturb them.

He led her up the stairs and across the floor, avoiding

the scattered pillows and rugs, and there at the far side of
the barn was a window. He knelt down and opened it
wide, letting in the moonlight and the teasing wind. A
carpet had been laid there, and he gathered together some
cushions and laid them down by the window, then knelt
on them, drawing her down beside him.

'Let me love you, Molly,' he breathed.

There were no words. Nothing needed saying.

She was wearing that dress again, the soft, draping crinkle-cotton dress with little flowers scattered all over it like
a wild meadow. He slid his hand up and cupped her bottom, drawing her closer. She was warm and yielding, her
hands trembling on his clothes, stripping them away until
they both lay naked in the moonlight.

He loved her with his hands, with his mouth, finally
with his body, covering her and losing himself in the ten-
derness of her arms.

She cried out, and he covered her mouth with his, trap-
ping the sound. He felt the shudder start deep inside him,
the building of the wave, the hard, pulsing tide of release.

And then he remembered, with the icy clarity of hind-
sight, the advice he'd given to Seb...

The wind teased her skin, cool and fresh, making her
shiver. Jack drew her closer. 'We ought to go back inside,'
he murmured.

'Mmm.'

She didn't want to move. She was comfortable on their
makeshift bed, and Jack's solid warmth kept the wind at
bay. She cupped his cheek.

'That was wonderful,' she told him.

His face was troubled.

'What?' she asked.

'You remember all that advice I gave Seb?'

'About—oh, Lord.'

She rolled onto her back and stared at the rafters. She hadn't given it a thought! And it was her most fertile time.

'I'll go to the doctor and get some pills—morning-after pills,' she said.

'It's Sunday tomorrow.'

'I'll get them on Monday. You have seventy-two hours, apparently. That should be OK.'

'You sure?'

She nodded. 'Of course.'

'You will tell me—if anything happens? If you're pregnant?'

A little shiver of wonder ran over her skin, but she suppressed it. *Seven* children?

Not even she was that mad.

'I'll tell you, but it won't happen. It can't. The tablets work.'

'But if not—'

'I'll tell you,' she promised.

They dressed and closed the window, throwing the cushions back where they'd been, and went back inside after a lingering kiss outside the front door.

Jack vanished into his bedroom, and she went along to hers and sat on the edge of the bed.

It was nearly four-thirty—her usual time to get up during the week. Even at the weekends, she had to get up at six. She thought of going to bed and then getting up again in an hour, and decided it was crazy. The garage was open all night. She'd go home now, make the sandwiches, deliver them and come back. She'd probably still get a couple of hours before they all got up.

She tapped on Jack's bedroom door, and he opened it, dressed only in a pair of briefs.

'Molly—'

'I'm going to go and do my sandwiches,' she told him in a soft undertone.

'OK.' He drew her into his arms and kissed her tenderly. 'Take care. I'll see you soon. Go to bed when you get back, have a lie-in. You looked bushed. I should have let you sleep.'

'I'm fine. I feel wonderful. I'll see you later.'

She kissed him again and slipped out of his arms, closing the door softly behind her. She was halfway down the stairs when she saw the movement, just the slightest shift of Seb's bedroom door.

Had he seen them? They didn't need any more complications, she thought, although if her morning-after pill failed, they'd all know in the end anyway.

It wouldn't fail. She'd take it exactly according to the instructions.

It couldn't fail.

What if the pills failed? Jack quelled the little flicker of hope. You're mad, Haddon, he told himself. Quite crazy. Life's complicated enough as it is.

He listened for Nicky, and smiled. His youngest complication was sitting with Boy watching television in the snug.

'Are you all right, darling?' he called.

'Want a biscuit,' she announced.

'OK, in a minute. Let me just do this.'

He was going over the love scene, replaying it in his mind, changing things.

The bed was under the open window; it was moonlight.

He found the words weren't adequate to express the way he'd felt with Molly, and had to remind himself that he wasn't writing about him and Molly, but about Toby and Maddy. What did it matter what they felt?

But it did matter, because they were real to him—and, if he was going to get paid, they had to be real to his editor, and to his readers.

He read the scene through again and tweaked some more.

'Want a biscuit.'

'Coming.'

The breeze caught the muslin curtain, trailing it over his skin with the touch of a lover. Maddy knelt up and tied the curtain out of the way, and he lay there and looked at her, silvered by the moonlight, the smooth curve of her hip—

There was a crash from the kitchen.

'Nicky?'

''s OK. It fell.'

What fell?

His hand reached up and caught her, drawing her down so that the soft skin of her midriff was by his face. He grazed it with his teeth-

'Jack, I can't—'

She started to cry, and he pushed slowly back from the computer and spun the chair round. 'Nicky? Where are you, sweetheart?'

'In the kitchen. Want a biscuit—'

'I'm coming.'

*   *   *

'Have you given any thought to any other form of contraception?' the doctor asked her, tapping away on his keyboard.

'Um—we don't have the chance to be together very often, so it seems a bit unnecessary taking the pill,' she began.

He peered at her over the top of his half-moon glasses and made a 'hmm' noise.

'This was different,' she explained hastily.

'It always is,' he assured her. 'It always is. How about—?' and he began listing a whole range of methods and devices which made her blood run cold.

It had been so wonderful just making love to Jack without thinking, with no barriers between them, so that she wasn't sure where she ended and he began.

She made noises about promising to think, and took the prescription. She'd get it at the supermarket.

Monday was a big shop always, because she didn't shop on Sunday and so her stocks of everything were low. She loaded all the things into the car, remembered her prescription and went back. It took ages, and she was worried about the chilled food simmering gently in the car.

Finally the pharmacist came back from her break, made up the prescription and handed it to her as she stood in the queue, giving her loud and precise instructions for taking it and what to expect afterwards.

'Thanks,' she gabbled, grabbed the packet and fled, her face flaming.

She arrived home to the ringing of the phone, and, running inside, she picked up the receiver.

'Molly?'

Fear trickled down her spine. 'Jack? What's wrong?'

'It's Nicky. She's fallen—we're in hospital, and she's having tests.' His voice shook. 'Molly, I need you.'

'Hang on, I'm coming,' she promised.

'It's not urgent. She's not dying. I just wanted to talk to you. I needed to hear your voice.'

'I'm coming,' she said again, and, dropping the phone, she ran back out to the car, grabbed the frozen and chilled food and piled it hastily away, then left the rest.

Nicky was much, much more important.

And Jack needed her.

Frankly, nothing else mattered.

CHAPTER NINE

SHE shook all the way to the hospital. It was two-thirty, and she had to get back to get the children by three-thirty, but she had to see him, to make sure he was all right, to comfort him. Nicky was in the best hands, but Jack needed her.

And what about his other three? Oh, Lord.

She turned into the hospital car park, pulled up in a space and ran to get a ticket, fumbling for change. What a time to have to find money, she thought crossly. She pulled the ticket out of the machine, stuck it in the car and ran for the Accident and Emergency entrance.

'I'm looking for Mr Haddon,' she told a nurse.

'Haddon? Sorry, I don't know if we've got anyone in here by that name. Have you checked in at Reception?'

'No. Actually, it's his daughter, Nicky. She's two. She fell.'

The nurse shook her head. 'No Nicky Haddon, sorry. Are you sure it was this hospital?'

Molly panicked. Had she got the wrong hospital? Oh, help—

'Selenka,' she said, suddenly remembering the painting on the kitchen wall. 'Nicky Selenka?'

'Oh, yes. Dad's called Jack, I think.'

'That's right,' she said, the tension draining away. 'Can I see him?'

'Are you Molly?'

She smiled with relief. 'Yes. That's right.'

The nurse returned her smile. 'I'm so glad you're here.

148

He's torturing himself—says it was his fault. But kids do
these things. Perhaps you can help him understand that.'

She showed Molly into a treatment room. Nicky was
lying on the bed, a cluster of doctors and nurses gathered
round her, and Jack was standing by her head, stroking it
and talking to her.

He looked up and his face crumpled for a second. She
crossed over to him, hugged him and looked down at
Nicky. She had a huge egg on her temple, and the doctors
were flashing lights in her eyes and talking to her, taking
her blood pressure, asking her to count fingers.

She seemed tired and fratchy but otherwise all right,
and Molly dropped a little kiss on her forehead in a mo-
mentary lull. 'Hello, sweetheart.'

'Molly,' she said sleepily. 'Nicky sick.'

'Lots of times,' Jack said drily.

She looked up into his strained face and smiled. 'How
are things?'

He shrugged. 'Inconclusive at the moment. It's nothing
drastic, I don't think. They're talking about keeping her
in overnight.'

'Yes, we will have to,' the doctor told them. 'Just for
observation. Her pupils are a little uneven and she's got
several symptoms of concussion, but the X-ray was clear.
We'll scan her later if we're concerned, but I don't think
we will be. She's been a lucky girl.'

He smiled at Nicky, patted her shoulder and went out,
leaving the nurses monitoring her. She dozed off, and Jack
drew Molly to one side and hugged her.

'Oh, I needed you so much. Thank you for coming.'

'Don't be silly. What happened?'

'She wanted a biscuit, and I was working. I kept saying
I was coming, and then there was this crash, and she'd
tried to climb up on the worktop to get them down and

fallen. She'd built a tower of tins to stand on on the worktop, pulled a chair over to get up on and somehow got
almost there before the tins tottered.' He shuddered.

'Resourceful little minx.'

'Absolutely. I should have known she'd gone too quiet.
I went out there just as she fell. I saw her fall but there
was nothing I could do—'

He screwed his eyes shut and bit his lips, and she put
her arms round him and hugged him. 'Jack, she'll be all
right. She'll just have a shocking headache, that's all.'

'But it's my fault—'

'No. She should have known better.'

'She's two,' he said harshly. 'I should have been watching her!'

Molly sighed. 'Probably, but we all have to compro-
mise. We've all taken our eye off them from time to time.
You can't watch their every move, Jack. Life's risky.'

'Not that risky.'

'Yes. She's not a baby of nine months that you've left
unattended on a worktop. She's a busy, active little girl
with a vivid imagination and a sense of adventure. She'll
know better next time.'

'God, I hope so,' he said on a sigh.

Molly squeezed his arm. 'She will. Look, what about
the others?'

He shook his head to clear it. 'Um—Seb gets home
about four-thirty on the bus. The others will get back a
little earlier and wonder where I am, but they know where
the key is. They should be OK.'

'For the night?'

His eyes widened. 'I forgot the night. No, not really for
the night. Molly—?'

'I'll take mine over there and stay with them.'

'But what about your sandwiches?'

'I'll make them at yours—or leave the children with Seb and go and do it, then go back. That's probably easier. They'll have to get themselves up, if you're happy for me to do that?'

'That's fine. They can get up without you, if Seb's there. Here.' He reached into his pocket and gave her his car keys. 'Use my car. It's insured for any driver—just be careful. It's bigger than yours, but at least you'll get them all in it.'

'You're very trusting,' she said, wondering if she'd be able to manage the huge vehicle. 'I'll bring them to visit you this evening.'

'If you can. Bring us some clothes—I'll need pyjamas and Nicky needs something clean to wear tomorrow and I expect she'd like her own PJs as well.'

'OK. I'll see you later. I'll ring before I bring the kids.'

She reached up and kissed him, blew a kiss to the sleeping child and went out. Her legs were trembling, but it was just reaction. Nicky was all right.

She went home, unpacked her shopping, gathered her brood and their clothes and went over to Jack's, just as Seb rolled up on his bike.

'Hi, Molly!' he called.

'Hi. Seb, can I talk to you?'

He stopped, searching her grave face, and his own went chalk-white. 'What's happened?' he croaked.

'Nicky's bumped her head. She seems OK, but they're keeping her in overnight, and Jack's staying with her.'

'Cripes. Do the others know?'

'Not yet.'

'We'd better tell them—can we go and see her?'

'I said I'd ring and make sure, but, yes, I'm certain we can. We're staying with you for the night, and Jack's given me the keys of his car. Let's just hope I can manage to drive it.'

They went in and told the other two, and predictably Amy burst into tears. 'I want to see her,' she sobbed, and so Molly rang the hospital, spoke to the sister on the children's ward and was told it was all right to take them in.

'Right, we'll go in a little while. All of you get something to eat and drink, and I'll find some clothes for them both.'

Seb appeared at her side as she reached the landing. 'I'll get Jack's stuff,' he said. 'I know what he needs.'

She shot him a smile. 'Thanks, Seb.'

He returned the smile with a quick one of his own, and then hesitated. 'Molly?'

'Yes?'

'She is all right, isn't she?'

Molly saw the fear in his eyes, and without thinking she hugged him. 'She's fine, Seb. She's fine, really. Don't worry.'

She let him go and he gulped and flashed her a smile of thanks, then went into the bedroom. She went into Nicky's room and found her things, then went down to round up the others just as Seb appeared with a bag for Jack.

'OK?' she asked. 'Have you got wash things? A razor?'

He nodded. 'I think I've got everything. Can we go?'

She screwed up her courage, started Jack's car and then looked at the gear lever. Automatic. Wonderful. All she had to do was point and brake. Thank goodness for that. At least she couldn't stall it!

'Right, kids,' she said with false cheer, and pulled away.

Nicky was in a little room, in a big cot with the sides half down, sleeping. Jack was sitting on a big vinyl chair with wooden arms, his head resting on the edge of the locker, one arm draped over the cot side holding Nicky's tiny hand.

Amy, Tom and Seb were in front of Molly, her own two behind. They didn't want to disturb Nicky, but her sister and brothers needed to see her.

Jack looked up when they went in, and, easing his hand away, he came over to them and hugged the two younger ones. 'Hi, kids,' he said wearily.

'Is she all right?' Amy asked anxiously.

'Yes, she's fine. She's just sleeping it off. They're quite happy with her now.'

He looked over their heads to Seb, and, reaching out a hand, he drew him into the hug. Seb hesitated for a moment, then his arms went up and he hugged them all, Jack as well, his hands lying along Jack's arms and gripping tight.

'It's OK, Seb, she'll be fine,' he said softly, and the boy's shoulders drooped with relief.

They broke apart, and the children tiptoed over to the side of the cot, peering down at Nicky.

'That's a wicked bruise,' Tom said in awe.

Molly's mouth curved in a smile, and Jack reached for her and hugged her hard, then hugged her children.

'Thanks for bringing them. You're a star, Molly.'

'I've got your clothes—well, the kids have. Hope we've got everything you need. Seb found your things.'

Jack nodded, took the bags and put them on the other bed in the room. It didn't look anything like long enough for him, but she knew he would rather be there hanging off the end than anywhere else in the world right now.

They didn't stay long, the children talking in muffled

undertones, and Nicky slept through it all, hardly stirring even when a nurse came in and took her blood pressure.

'We'd better go. We haven't had supper and they might have homework. I know it's nearly the end of term, but you never can tell. Oh, what's your childminder's number? I'd better let her know.'

'It's in the book—Helen. Seb'll find it. Bless you, Molly.'

They left the two of them there in the dim light of the little room, and went home. She felt more confident now in the big people carrier, and was actually quite enjoying the high driving position.

'OK?' Seb asked her, watching her curiously.

'Yes. It's rather nice.'

'It's easy to drive. Jack lets me take it up and down the track sometimes.'

It didn't surprise her. He was good at knowing when the time was right for things. Even though he wasn't a father, he was doing a very good job of it, she thought, and nobody seeing him with Nicky, the worry on his face, would doubt that she was his.

She just hoped the little one really was all right and that they were worrying for nothing.

Four o'clock seemed to come awfully early the next morning. She went home, made her orders, left them on the side in the cool room and went back to the children.

They were up, wandering apparently aimlessly round the kitchen getting their breakfasts.

'Jack rang,' Seb told her. 'Nicky's fine.'

'Oh, good.' How irrational, to be so disappointed to have missed his call. 'I've brought you sandwiches for your lunches,' she told them, and was greeted with sighs of relief from Jack's brood. She dished them out, settled the children down at the table to finish eating and then sent them off to their various buses before setting off with her two in the car to deliver them to school, fetch the sandwiches and go to work.

She felt exhausted by the time she'd finished, the strain of yesterday catching up with her, and she got back to find Jack and Nicky in the snug.

'You're home!' she said in delight, and he nodded.

'We got a taxi. You weren't here, and I assumed you'd still be at work. Everything OK? Were the kids good?'

'Fine. Hi, Nicky, how are you, darling? You look much better.'

'Got bruise,' she said cheerfully. 'Fell down. Want a biscuit.'

'I'll get it,' Jack said firmly, and opened one of the bottom cupboards to take a biscuit from the tin.

'I thought that lived at the top?'

'It used to,' he said flatly. 'Here, sweetheart.'

'Want a chocolate one.'

'No chocolate ones. Anyway, you'll be sick again. Here.'

She took it and ate it without fuss, and Jack left her there on the sofa with Boy, watching television, while they went into the kitchen next door.

'Coffee?' Molly offered.

He was propped against the worktop at the end of the kitchen, keeping an eye on Nicky through the open door. 'Sounds good,' he murmured distractedly.

'Jack, she's fine.'

He sighed and nodded. 'Yes. I know.'

'So relax.'

'I can't.'

'You must. How's the book?'

He tunnelled his fingers through his hair and sighed

again. 'Um—OK, I think. Almost finished. I was just getting everything sorted ready for the run down to the end.
Another few hours, I suppose?'

'So why don't you have a drink and some lunch, and
then go and get on with it?'

'What about Nicky?'

'I'll watch her.'

'But you have to shop.'

'I can shop later when the others are home from school.
I'll stay till you finish it.'

He stared at her for a long time, then with one stride
he was across the room, enveloping her in a huge hug. 'I
love you, Molly, you're wonderful,' he said, and her heart
kicked crazily.

'Just finish the book,' she said, laughing, and turned
away. 'I've brought us the leftovers. What do you fancy?'

He hadn't meant it, she told herself. It was just a figure
of speech, something she often said jokingly if someone
did her a favour.

That was all.

No significance whatsoever.

Damn.

It was nearly midnight, and she and the children were all
safely tucked up in bed, when her door eased open and
Jack came in.

'OK?' she whispered, scooting up the bed and shoving
the hair out of her eyes.

'I've finished,' he murmured, and she could hear the
suppressed excitement in his voice. 'I've done it, Molly.
Thank you.'

His arms came round her and he drew her against his
chest, then kissed her. It was a gentle kiss, a kiss of

thanks, not a passionate one that threatened their self-control.

Not the kiss of a man in love.

Molly squeezed him hard and let go. 'So, what happens now?'

'I print off the last bit, read it all through, throw it in the post and my editor will tear it to bits and send it back for rejigging.'

And you won't need me any more.

Oh, God, no.

'That's great,' she murmured. 'I'm so glad you've done it.' She faked a yawn, and he tutted and stood up.

'I'm sorry, I've woken you. I'll see you in the morning.'

He went out, closing the door softly behind him, and she lay down, turned her face into the pillow and wept.

The following morning she went and made her sandwiches, came back for her children and left Jack to it.

He kissed her goodbye on the cheek, because the children were there, and thanked her yet again. 'Bless you, Molly,' he murmured, and let her go. She took the children to school, delivered her orders and went home, sitting down quietly with a cup of tea.

Well, she might see him again with the children, of course, but he hadn't said anything about contacting her.

And as for that 'I love you'!

'Oh, Jack,' she whispered brokenly. 'We could have had so much.'

She wallowed for a minute, then put her cup down and went to clear up. The place was still in chaos from the other day, and some of the shopping, tins and things, still hadn't been put away properly.

She went to sort it out, and in the bottom of one of the bags she found a little pharmacy packet.

'Oh, Lord.'

A cold chill ran over her.

She hadn't taken the pills. In all the confusion over Nicky, she'd forgotten all about it.

She sat down on the kitchen floor with a plop, and opened the packet, reading the instructions aloud.

'"Take two tablets as soon as possible after intercourse, within seventy-two hours. Take the other two exactly twelve hours later." Oh, damn. It's too late.'

Except that it had been on Sunday morning, really, and it was only Wednesday morning. Monday, Tuesday, Wednesday. Seventy-two hours, give or take. It might work.

She stood up, took the first two pills and put the others under her quilt so she'd remember when she went to bed.

Not that there was any danger of forgetting them. She thought about nothing else all day.

Everything got back to normal after that. A day later the schools broke up for the summer and the kids were off to Holiday Club every morning.

Despite Tom's pleading she'd only been able to arrange for her two to join the others in their Holiday Club on a few occasions, but perhaps that was just as well.

She was busy, because it was the wedding season, and on top of her usual orders she had wedding buffets in her diary nearly every week.

She had a period—just a very light one, a few days early, but she heaved a sigh of relief anyway. Jack hadn't contacted her, and she was beginning to feel that he'd simply used her when he'd needed her—at home, when Nicky was in hospital, when he was writing—when he was frustrated.

It didn't stop her loving him, and it didn't stop her missing him or his children.

It just made the hurt even deeper, but what had she expected? She hadn't managed to hold David, and they had two children! What chance did she have with Jack?

And then one day he turned up out of the blue with Nicky in tow.

She was struggling with a wedding cake, putting the finishing touches to the icing, and she went to the door and opened it.

Did jaws literally drop? She thought so. She was sure hers did. She opened the door wider and smiled, unable to help herself.

'Hello, Jack. Hello, Nicky. How's your bump?' she asked.

'Better.' She pulled her hand out from behind her back and thrust a colourful little posy of sweet peas at her. 'Thank you for lookin' after me,' she said shyly, and Molly gave a strangled laugh and crouched down to hug her.

'Oh, darling, you're welcome! Oh, they're lovely, thank you.'

She tilted her head back and looked up at Jack. 'Thanks,' she said with a smile, and he helped her up, his hand warm and firm on her arm.

'It's nothing. Nicky wanted to bring you something.' He looked awkward. 'Are you busy?'

'Not especially,' she lied. 'Want a coffee?'

'I'd love one.'

She took them in the garden, because it was a lovely day, and Nicky chased the cat and had fun in the sandpit that Tom had loved when he was younger. It was a bit green around the gills, but Molly found her a trowel and a flowerpot, and she was soon making sandcastles.

'We ought to go to the beach one day,' he said.

'I haven't got time. I've got some weddings coming up, and I have to make the cakes and all the food.'

'Surely you could spare one day?'

It was so tempting.

'I'll look in my diary. I might be able to wangle half a day.'

If I work all night.

I want to be with him! she wanted to scream, but she was too sensible. Just.

'Try,' he coaxed, and she met his eyes and wondered if she'd been wrong, or if he'd just been busy too, like her.

Nicky left the sandpit and ran up the garden after a butterfly.

'I've missed you,' he said softly, when she was out of earshot. 'It seems odd without you around, but I really felt I ought to give the children time. Things have been a bit hectic recently, and I wanted us to get back to normal.'

He studied his hands for a moment. 'Um—those pills you took.'

'They worked,' she said, and wondered if she'd dreamt it or if there'd been a flicker of sadness on his face. 'So you don't have to worry. You can get back to normal and forget it ever happened.'

'I'll never forget you happened, Molly.'

Oh, Lord, that sounded so final. A huge pain wedged itself in her chest and nearly made her cry out.

'I'm sorry to hustle you, but I've got a cake to finish before I pick the children up.'

'What about the beach? Can you look in your diary?'

'I don't think I'll have time,' she said firmly.

'Can I take the kids?'

'Six of them, on your own? That's probably not safe.'

He sighed. 'OK. Thanks for the coffee.' He stood up and called Nicky, and she came running down the garden all smiles.

Molly felt her eyes prickle. She hugged the little girl, kissed Jack's cheek and showed them out, then, closing the door behind them, she leant on the wall, slid down it and crumpled at the bottom.

'Oh, damn!' she whispered, and then the tears fell…

So the pills had worked.

Damn.

Jack stood in the barn, looking out of the window where he and Molly had made love, and felt a huge sadness engulf him. It was a gorgeous day. The kids were all playing outside, keeping a close eye on Nicky, and he'd slipped up to the top of the barn for a few moments alone with his thoughts.

Not that it was doing him any good.

'You're a fool, Haddon,' he muttered for the hundredth time. 'Four kids is enough.'

But it would have been mine.

He swallowed the pain, forcing it down, and propped his arm against the window frame.

'They're all yours,' he reminded himself, remembering the promise he'd made Nick on his deathbed, that he'd look after Jan and the children.

'I'll guard them with my life, Nick, you know that. I'll keep them safe.'

'It's a lot to ask.'

'It won't come to that. You're going to get better.'

'If I don't—'

'Then I'll look after them all as if they're my own.'

And he had, and he had vowed that he would never regret it.

He didn't, not really, but it had been too much for Molly. When he'd realised what they'd done that night, and told her, she'd been very quick to say she was going to the doctor. Clearly the idea of marrying him, taking on the children and having more filled her with horror.

It filled him with horror, too, but there was a bit of him a mile wide that wanted it more than he wanted to breathe.

'You're mad.'

Anyway, there was no baby, and there wouldn't be. No child of his and Molly's, no one to carry his name, no son or daughter to look up at him with his own eyes and call him Daddy.

Tears clogged his throat, and he closed his eyes and called himself a sentimental fool.

It wasn't just the child, though. A baby would have meant Molly. Fate might have guided them together, but he couldn't ask her to marry him and take on that much responsibility.

It was just as well it had worked out like this.

I miss you, his heart cried, and he gritted his teeth and choked back the tears.

'Jack?'

Seb. Hell. He straightened up and blinked. Hopefully, in the half-light of the barn— 'What is it? Did you want me?'

'Just wondered where you were. You OK?'

'Yeah, I'm fine.' Just dying inside.

'It's lunchtime. The kids are hungry. I wondered if we should do beans on toast or something.'

'Sounds good. I'm coming down now. I was just enjoying the view.' He turned round and gave Seb the ghost of a smile. 'I suppose we ought to take these rugs back inside to keep them dry—the roof leaks in places if it rains hard.'

'Shall we do it after lunch?'

'Sure. Give me a hand?'

Seb nodded and smiled at him warily. Did it show? The awful wretchedness he felt without Molly?

It seemed unbelievable that it might not.

He saw her a few days later, at Holiday Club. She was dropping Cassie and Tom off, and she looked harassed.

'Molly? Are you all right?'

She smiled distractedly at him. 'Just about. I've got a wedding tomorrow, and I'm way behind.'

He was a fool, but then he knew that. 'Let me have them for you for the night—let you get on.'

She stared at him. 'Oh, but I couldn't!'

'Why? You did it enough times for me.'

Her eyes softened and filled. 'Oh, Jack, would you? It would make so much difference if I didn't have to worry about them.'

'That's agreed, then. I'll pick them up from here, and you can fetch them when you've finished. Don't worry about clothes and things; I'm sure I can find them something and we've got some new toothbrushes somewhere. You just go and get on.'

She gave a relieved smile. 'Thank you,' she whispered, and then looked at the door. 'I ought to tell them.'

'I can tell them.'

'I ought to.' She went in, and emerged a moment later. 'OK?'

She nodded. 'Didn't you hear the shriek of delight?'

He laughed, watching her climb into her car and shoot off down the road, and his heart ached.

You're a masochist, he told himself, and, getting into the car, he drove home and started dreaming up something nice for supper.

*   *   *

'Right, I cooked; you lot clear up, please.'

'Oh, Jack!'

'Come on, you guys,' Seb said firmly. 'It won't take long.'

Jack sent him a smile of thanks over their heads, and went into the study. He'd had the book back with rave reviews from his editor, and he only had to make a few minor changes.

He'd even liked the love scene!

Jack decided he couldn't be bothered with it tonight, and so he shut down the computer, opened the study door and went through to the snug. The kitchen door was open, and he was about to turn on the television when he heard Amy speaking.

'I wish we had a mum,' she said sadly, and Jack froze.

'*I* wish we had a dad,' Cassie replied. 'Jack's so nice, and he really cares about you. Our dad went off to Australia so he didn't have to bother with us.'

All the pain in those few short words. Jack ached for them. At least the Selenkas had loved their children and wanted to be there for them.

'Jack's not really our father,' Tom said. 'We had a real father, but he died.'

'I know. Mum told us.' That was Philip.

'I reckon Jack's a real father,' Seb said softly. 'He may not really be ours, but he loves us just as much as a real father would.'

Oh, hell. His eyes were filling up again. What was it about this week that was determined to make him cry?

'I'd *hate* not to have a mother,' Cassie said slowly. 'If our mum died, I don't know what I'd do.'

'You'd have to find a Jack.'

'Maybe our Jack would have you.'

And he knew, without a second's hesitation, that he would.

Perhaps he ought to go and work for Barnado's?

Then Amy said something that stopped him in his tracks.

'Hey, wouldn't it be cool if they got married?'

CHAPTER TEN

MOLLY picked the children up the following evening, but she didn't come in. She looked exhausted, and Jack wanted to take her in his arms and tell her she'd never have to work again—just live there with them all in absolute chaos!

'Thank you so much,' she said wearily. 'I only just got done as it was.'

'Did you sleep?'

She shook her head. 'Not really. I went to bed, but I was so afraid I'd oversleep I didn't dare. Have you heard about the book?'

'Yes—he likes it, thanks to you. It wouldn't have got written without your help.'

'I'm sure it would—just during the night.'

He felt his mouth twitch in a smile. 'Probably. Anyway, thanks. I'm sure the kids would be grateful. I'm foul when I'm overtired.'

She laughed. 'I know the feeling. Come on, kids, time to go. Say goodbye.'

She had to drag them out, almost. They were most reluctant to leave, and he thought about what they'd all been saying the night before, and wondered if he dared ask Molly to marry him.

Then he remembered how quick she'd been to make sure there was no baby, and he thought better of it. There was no point in exposing himself to any further hurt.

Anyway, she was piling the kids into the car and staying carefully out of reach. She hugged the others, even Seb, and then threw him a little wave.

'Bye, Jack. Thanks again.'

And then they were gone.

She hadn't even hugged him!

He caught himself feeling left out, and stomped on it fast. Damn it, it was ridiculous the way he was behaving. He wasn't one of the kids, and anyway, in front of them, it was quite right for her to act with a little circumspection. No point in building their hopes up.

'Who wants to go to the beach tomorrow?' he asked, and they all looked at him.

'Yeah, OK,' Tom said.

'You don't sound very keen.'

Amy's eyes trailed down the drive after Molly, and she shrugged. 'Can we take Cassie and Philip?'

'No. Molly's too busy and she doesn't want me taking six of you on my own. She says it's too much responsibility. Anyway, wouldn't it be nice to do something with just the five of us together?'

Amy shrugged again, Tom pulled a face and Seb wandered off. Only Nicky showed any enthusiasm.

'Go to the beach,' she said eagerly. 'Make sandcastles.'

'We could have a picnic,' he said, following them in and trying to sound enthusiastic.

Seb pulled a face. 'You just get sand in the sandwiches.'

'That's why they're called sand-wiches,' Amy said importantly. 'Anyway, they won't be Molly's. I like Molly's best.'

'We could buy them from the garage in the morning, on the way.'

They looked a little brighter, and he sighed. Was he

going to be reduced to bribing them with Molly's food to get them to do anything? Suddenly being a parent seemed a very hard thing to do…

The morning was a little dull and overcast, but the forecast was good, and Jack set about packing up all their things for the beach in plenty of time. He was determined that they were going to have a successful family day, and he would make sure they would if it killed him.

He shut Boy in the outside run they used if they went out for a long time, gave him a bone, and loaded them all into the car.

The first hiccup was Molly's sandwiches. When they stopped at the garage, they found that there were only a few left.

'No egg and cress!' Amy said.

'And no tuna and mayonnaise,' Seb said with a sigh. 'Tom, what did you want?'

'Ham salad.'

'Sorry. There's cheese salad—or chicken tikka.'

'Ugh, yuck.' Tom curled his lip.

'I'll have that,' Jack said, taking it from Seb. 'I think we'd better just have a variety and make the best of it.'

In the end they almost cleaned them out, leaving only the cheese and pickle that none of them liked.

It was the first of many hiccups.

When they arrived at the beach, the car park had a low barrier to prevent camper-vans from going in, and it was too low for the people carrier to fit underneath, so they had to park some distance away in a side-road and walk back.

'Look on the bright side, at least it's free,' Seb said cheerfully.

'I would rather have paid,' Jack muttered, struggling

under the cool box, the windbreak and a couple of swimming bags. 'I don't suppose you lot could make yourselves useful and carry something, could you?'

'We're all carrying things already,' Amy pointed out.

Seb was holding Nicky's hand and carrying his swimming bag and a body board, and Nicky was carrying her bucket and spade in the other hand. She kept dropping them, and they had to stop frequently while she retrieved them, but she wouldn't let Seb help.

Amy had her own bag and a beach umbrella, Tom had his bag, a body board and flippers, and so Jack reined in his sigh and struggled on.

Then Amy fell down the last few steps and scraped her knee, and cried, and they had to take her to the stand pipe outside the ladies' and wash it out. It was sore and needed a plaster, but they were in the car.

Seb, with a resigned sigh, went back for them and came back with the news that the car had a ticket on it.

'What?' Jack yelled, and then got a grip on his frustration. 'How come?'

'It's a residents' parking zone,' Seb said. 'It says so on the little sign by the car. We missed it. Oh, well, you said you'd rather have paid.'

He closed his eyes, counted to ten and put the plaster on Amy's knee. Then Nicky needed the loo and Amy hobbled into the ladies' with her.

'Somebody wee'd on the seat,' Nicky announced as they came out. 'I sat in it.'

Jack closed his eyes again and counted to twenty this time. 'I don't suppose it'll kill you,' he told her, and then caught Seb's eye. He was leaning against the sea wall laughing, and Jack scowled at him and grabbed Nicky's hand. 'Right, let's go and find somewhere to sit.'

The beach was heaving, crazy since the sky was still a

little overcast, but it was quite a warm day and they were all in their cosy little beach huts, anyway, with their kettles, making tea.

What he wouldn't give for a quiet cup of tea!

It got worse before it got better. Nicky dropped her sandwich in the sand, Tom stepped in something nasty left by a careless dog owner and screamed until Jack had sorted it out and cleaned it up, and there weren't enough beach bunnies around for Seb to oggle.

'No talent at all,' he said with disgust.

Jack laughed. 'I thought you had Alison?'

'I do. Doesn't mean I'm blind.'

Funny, Jack thought, since he'd met Molly he'd hardly noticed another woman. Maybe age made all the difference. Perhaps when Seb was thirty-six he wouldn't notice women either.

Jack thought he would have noticed Molly at ninety-six, but never mind.

'I want to go in the sea,' Tom announced. 'Seb?'

'Nah—too cold.'

'Jack?' he asked hopefully.

Jack sighed. It had been his idea to come to the beach, and he could hardly refuse to let Tom go in the water after all the coercion. 'OK. Seb, can you watch Nicky for a minute? Put some sunblock on her.'

'It's cloudy.'

'It's hazy. You can still burn. Just do it, please—and watch my wallet.'

He took Seb's body board and followed Tom down to the water. 'Hell's teeth!' he exclaimed as a wave rushed in and curled like ice around his ankles.

'It's fine—you'll be all right in a minute.'

That sounded familiar, he thought. How many times had he told them that?

He took a deep, bolstering breath and ran in, hurling himself into the water. He felt his body recoil with shock, and his lungs locked up and refused to work for a moment.

He turned, launched himself onto the body board and surfed up the beach onto the gravel. His knees graunched on the stones, and he stood up, watching in disgust as thin trickles of blood oozed out of the skin and ran in tiny rivulets down his legs.

'Tom, mind your knees,' he called, turning round, just as Tom came flying up the beach and chopped him in the legs with the body board.

'Ow!' he yelled, dropping to the stones and grabbing his ankles.

'Sorry,' Tom said cheerfully. 'This is cool—you coming in again?'

Jack gave a despairing little laugh. 'Yeah, sure,' he said, resigned, and, with the dedication worthy of a saint, he re-entered the water.

He had just decided he'd had enough when Amy wanted to come in. Nicky and Seb came down to the edge and Nicky screamed and giggled when it splashed her. 'Can I have your body board?' Amy asked, taking it, and he was left with nothing to do and freezing to bits.

'Where's my wallet?' he asked Seb, and the boy's face was comical.

'Um—watch Nicky,' he yelled, and legged it up the beach. Just before he reached their pitch he crumpled, grabbing his foot, and Jack was torn between watching Amy and Tom, and seeing what had happened to Seb.

In the end he split the difference and went halfway,

Nicky firmly clamped to the end of his arm, head swivelling to watch both camps.

'What have you done?' he called.

'Trodden on a shell,' Seb said, fighting back tears. 'Ouch. Your wallet's still here, though.'

His shoulders sagged with relief, and he took Nicky up the beach to Seb, handed her over to him and looked at his foot. It was bleeding freely, and he looked a bit green. If it wasn't one thing, it was another.

'I'll get the others out of the water. Give it a good wash and I'll have a look at it in a minute. Hang onto Nicky.'

He went back down and called Tom and Amy, then went back up with them. It was a fairly nasty cut, a deep slice under the soft part of his foot, and it was obviously sore.

'I think we'd better call it a day,' Jack said, and packed up all the stuff. 'I'll get the car and we can load all this lot from the top. If you hobble up there and Amy and Tom carry the stuff, I'll take Nicky back to the car and come and collect you, OK?'

They nodded, and he set off with Nicky. The parking ticket on the windscreen was flapping gently under the windscreen wiper, and he snatched it off and stuffed it on the dashboard. Just one more irritation, he thought. He strapped Nicky in, went back for the others and loaded the things in while Seb limped up to the door and climbed in.

Thank God he hadn't brought Cassie and Philip as he'd suggested! Four was bad enough. Still, it was over now.

They were almost home when they had the puncture.

'Molly promised to take me bra shopping,' Amy said a few days later.

'I can take you bra shopping,' Jack said. 'We can go

to one of those places where they have special ladies to help do it.'

'I want Molly,' she said, looking horrified at the thought of a special lady. 'We were all going to go to the mall, and you were going to take Seb and Tom and Nicky, and Molly was going to take me and Cassie and do girly stuff.'

He sighed. 'I don't think we can ask Molly to do that. She's too busy.'

'But she promised!' Amy said, and ran out of the room in tears.

Oh, hell.

He debated ringing her, but then thought better of it. Amy didn't need a bra anyway. She only had gnat bites as yet. Surely there was plenty of time?

He was reading through the manuscript, painfully reminded of Molly with every gesture Maddy made, when the phone rang.

'Jack, it's Molly,' she said, as if he'd conjured her out of his imagination.

'Hello, Molly,' he said cautiously. Odd, how their spontaneous greetings had disappeared. 'What can I do for you?'

'Cassie's nagging me,' she said, straight to the point. 'I promised to take her and Amy shopping for bras, and I haven't done it. I wondered if it would be OK if I pick her up tomorrow morning and leave Philip with you? I can't take them to the mall, I haven't got time, but I have to go into town for a few bits and pieces, so it's not a problem to do that if it's OK with you.'

She ground to a halt, and he wondered if Amy had rung her. Probably, the little minx. 'Are you sure?'

'Yes, of course. The other thing is, have you done the

periods bit with her—bought the gear, told her how to use it?'

He felt his neck going warm. 'Um—no. I didn't think it was necessary yet.'

'Would you like me to? It's easier if a woman does it.'

He heaved a mental sigh of relief. 'Would you? It seems a dreadful imposition.'

'Jack, don't be daft,' she said with some of her old spark. 'I'll pick her up at ten-thirty, OK?'

'Great. Thanks, Molly.'

He cradled the phone and debated going to ask Amy if she knew anything about it, and decided it didn't matter. If Molly was happy to do it, it was better for Amy, and so he'd let it pass.

And anyway, he'd get to see her again.

What a bittersweet thought.

She found the girls some nice, sporty crop-top bras that would grow with them and give them adequate support in the meantime, and then she did her other shopping, including a detour into a chemist's shop.

She took the girls back home for lunch, then sat them both down and went over periods and all the attendant paraphernalia. She'd already touched on it with Cassie, but Amy had only done a certain amount at school, and clearly nobody had talked to her from a personal viewpoint.

'Mum told me a bit,' she said, 'but it was ages ago, and I can't really remember.'

So Molly gave them all the tips and hints she knew, told them stories about her own growing up, and generally prepared them as well as she could.

Then, horribly conscious of the time, she took Amy home and collected Philip, declining Jack's offer of a cup of tea. He was only being polite, and she couldn't bear to sit there and listen to them all chatter, and wish—

'You're a fool,' she muttered.

'What?'

'Nothing, darlings. Did you have a nice time with Tom?'

'We went down to the river with Boy and he went in the water. He came out *really* smelly.'

She sniffed and curled her nose. 'I wondered what it was.'

It was vile. She felt quite queasy with it, and opened her window. The fresh air helped a little, but not much.

'Go and put all those things in the basin, have a bath, and then throw them into the bathwater to soak for a while. We'll put them in the washing machine later.'

We. Hah. She went into the bathroom on her way to bed and the place was covered in reeking clothes. She felt the queasiness grab at her again, and shook her head. She was tired. Over-tired. She left the mess till the morning and went to bed, oversleeping for the first time in ages so that she had to rush and cut corners.

Slow, elaborate fillings got left off the list today, and tuna and mayonnaise and chicken tikka were high on the list, because they were easy. Even so, she was late and several of her customers grumbled.

She apologised and vowed to have some early nights. She couldn't afford to foul up her livelihood.

Jack called the dog and set off over the fields. Nicky was at the childminder, Amy and Tom were at Holiday Club and Seb had gone off on his bike. He was only halfway down the first field when Seb came back.

'Want to join me?' he called.

'Hang on, I'll get boots.'

He waited, Boy bouncing and chasing his tail, and then Seb came running over the field towards him.

'Where are you going?' he asked, a little breathless.

'Just down to the river, where I usually go. It's nice to have company for a change.'

'I would have thought you'd like a bit of peace and quiet,' Seb said with a laugh, falling in beside him. 'All of us lot around you all the time.'

'I don't mind you all,' he said. 'What made you think that?'

'The fact that we make you tear your hair out? The fact that you can't get on with anything because one of us is always underfoot? The fact that there's no privacy, that nothing's sacred, that if you put anything down it gets moved?'

Jack gave a rueful chuckle. 'Well, there is that, but look on the other side. I have company whenever I'm lonely, someone to talk to and share things with—'

'But not like a wife.'

Jack sighed. 'No. Not like a wife.'

Seb shoved his hands in his pockets and tromped down the hill in silence for a moment. Then he chewed his lip, lifted his head and said, 'Um—'

'Yes?' Jack prompted.

'Molly.'

He nearly choked. 'What about Molly?'

Seb shot him a searching look, then turned away again. 'I don't suppose you and Molly have thought about getting married?'

'No. No, Seb, we haven't.'

He kicked a tussock of grass in passing. 'Can I ask you something?'

'Sure,' he said, not at all sure he was going to like what was coming.

'Are you sleeping with her?'

Jack closed his eyes briefly and cast about for inspiration. 'Um—well, not exactly.'

'Not exactly sleeping? You know what I mean, Jack.'

'Yes, I do, and I'm not sure it's any of your business.'

Seb gave him a jaundiced look. 'Come on, Jack, I'm not twelve any more. I know what goes on.'

Jack sighed. Seb was right; he wasn't twelve, he wasn't his son, and having a relationship with another single parent was hardly going to destroy him as a role-model. He might as well tell the truth.

'Yes, we are. Well, we have done, but not recently.'

'I wondered.' Seb looked around. 'Um—Jack, I know I'm only a kid and all that, but you won't hurt her, will you?'

'What?' Jack stopped in his tracks, disbelief echoing in his voice. 'Is this one of those ''What are your intentions, my son?'' lectures?'

Seb gave a crooked grin. 'We all love Molly, Jack. We don't want her hurt—or you. But just recently you've both been looking sad, and she hasn't been around like she was at first.'

'There were reasons why she was there,' he said evasively.

'And now?'

Jack felt a huge weight in his chest. 'Now—the reasons aren't there. I've finished my book, Nicky's not in hospital, she's busy. She's got a lot of weddings to do the catering for. Anyway, are you complaining that I've got time for you or something?'

Seb gave a crooked grin. 'Of course not. We just miss her.'

Jack felt his face contort and looked hastily away. 'I

miss her too, Seb,' he said softly, 'but we can't always have everything we want.'

'You got on so well. We thought…'

Jack sighed. 'I know what you thought, Seb. I heard you all, the other night.'

'It would be really good, Jack.'

He swallowed. 'Maybe not for all of us,' he replied.

Seb was silent for a minute, then he shoved his hands in his pockets again and straightened his shoulders. Funny, the boy had grown up almost overnight and he'd hardly noticed. 'Is it us?' he asked bluntly.

'What?'

'Is it us? Is it because you've got us? I mean, if you didn't have any kids, would you ask her to marry you?'

Yes, he thought, but he couldn't tell Seb that.

'I don't know. I have got kids. I haven't even considered what I might do if I didn't have any.'

'I could look after them. We could go to Grannie and Grandpa, and come and stay with you in the holidays sometimes. I could help with the younger ones, and Amy's getting older; she could help too—'

'Hey, hey, stop,' Jack interrupted, catching hold of his shoulders and staring him straight in the eyes. 'What is this? Don't you want to be with me any more?'

Seb gulped and looked down. 'Of course we do, but if we're stopping you and Molly getting married, then it isn't fair.'

'Life isn't fair,' he said softly. 'Nobody ever said it was. Yes, I love Molly. Yes, I want to marry her, but I don't think she wants to marry me. And anyway, I love all of you, too. I couldn't possibly choose between all of you and Molly. I'd be gutted without you.'

Seb's eyes filled. 'Really?'

'Really. Come here,' he said gruffly, and, pulling the

boy into his arms, he hugged him hard. 'You're my best mate, Seb. I haven't had one since your father died, and you're so like him I could be talking to him sometimes. I wouldn't let anything get in the way of that.'

Seb stood for a moment, then his arms came round Jack and he hugged him back, just briefly. 'Thanks,' he mumbled, a little raggedly, and turned away, scrubbing his cheeks with the heels of his hands.

They turned back towards the house, and Jack whistled for the dog. He came, nose to the ground, tail wagging.

'Um—if Molly *did* want to marry you—'

'Seb, she doesn't.'

'You said you hadn't asked her.'

Jack shook his head. 'It's just certain things she's said—'

'But you haven't come right out and asked her?'

'No.'

'Does she know you love her?'

'I love you, Molly.'

'I don't know. Maybe.' If she'd listened, and hadn't just heard a meaningless social exchange instead of a declaration.

'Perhaps you ought to tell her.'

'Perhaps you ought to butt out, Seb. There are certain things a person has to do alone. This is one of them.'

Seb looked thoughtful. 'OK,' he said, but Jack had an uneasy feeling the subject wasn't closed.

Molly had just put the last of the shopping away and was sitting down for a well-earned cup of tea when the phone rang.

'Molly? It's Seb. Look, can you come over? It's Jack.'

Molly sat bolt upright. 'What's wrong with Jack?'

'Um—I don't know. He sort of collapsed—'

'I'm coming now. Call an ambulance.'

She slammed the phone down and called the children. 'Get in the car—Jack's sick,' she said, throwing her bag in and jumping in after it.

'How sick?' Cassie asked.

Molly tried again to get the key in the ignition. 'I don't know. Is the front door shut?'

'Yes. Mummy, he's not going to die, is he?'

Oh, God, no, she thought. Not Jack! He's so big and strong and alive—he can't die! He's too young!

'Of course not,' she flannelled. 'Oh, come on, come on—'

It went in, and she gunned the engine and shot off the drive, heading towards Jack. Hang on, my love, she thought. Hang on. I'm coming.

She made the journey in record time, skidding to a halt on the drive and jumping out, running to the door. Seb met her there, looking a little pale.

'He's in the study,' he said, and she ran through the kitchen, past the silent children, and through the study door.

Jack was sitting at his desk, head bent over his computer, tapping the keyboard.

Molly sagged against the doorpost and stared at him in disbelief. 'Jack?' she said weakly. 'Are you all right?'

He lifted his head and met her eyes, and then leapt to his feet and came round, taking her by the shoulders and steering her to a chair. 'Molly? What's the matter? You look dreadful.'

'Seb said—' she began weakly, and Jack rolled his eyes.

'Said what?'

Molly sagged back against the chair and stared at him,

hardly daring to believe he hadn't died. 'You really are all right? You would tell me if you'd collapsed?'

'Collapsed!' he exploded, and then he shut his eyes and started to laugh. 'Hell, Molly, I'm sorry. We've been set up. I'm sorry. Let me make you a cup of tea and you can go home—'

'How do you mean, set up? Who by? Why?'

The smile died in his eyes, and he sat down in his chair, scooting it over so it was opposite her. He took her hands, smoothing the soft skin with his thumbs and making her wish all sorts of things she shouldn't.

'Tell me, Jack,' she prompted gently. 'I thought you were dying. I think I deserve the truth.'

He nodded. 'They were all talking the other day about us getting married,' he began.

'All?' she croaked.

'When the kids were round here while you were doing the wedding. They were in the kitchen, and I overheard them. Then Seb had a little man-to-man chat with me yesterday, and asked me about you.'

'And you said?'

'That I love you. That I didn't think you'd want to marry me.'

Her eyes were locked on his, her heart pounding. 'And what did Seb say?'

Jack sighed and looked uncomfortable. 'That I ought to ask you—should let you decide.'

She searched his face, seeing the pain behind his eyes.

'And what do you want, Jack?' she asked quietly. 'Do you want to marry me?'

'Oh, God, yes,' he said raggedly. 'Molly, you know I do.'

She sighed with relief. 'No, I don't. I knew you cared a bit, but then I wondered if I'd just been convenient—'

'Convenient!' he exploded. 'Molly, I wouldn't do that! You thought I used you?'

'I wondered,' she said sadly. 'You seemed to switch off, all of a sudden.'

'You were in such a hurry to get to the doctor, as if the thought of another child was too much to tolerate. I hoped—oh, hell, I don't know what I hoped. Maybe that you'd get pregnant? That we'd have a child of our own to bring up together? God, I don't know, Molly. I need my head checked, but for a crazy moment I thought how wonderful that would be.'

She sat back and smiled. 'I hope it was more than a crazy moment, Jack, because the answer's yes—if you really are asking me to marry you.'

He stared at her, stunned. 'You mean you will? Marry me, and take on all these kids? That'll be six of them, Molly. Think very carefully.'

'Seven, actually,' she said softly. 'I forgot to take the pills until it was too late. We're going to have that baby, Jack.'

His face was a joy to watch. Disbelief, surprise, hope, love, all rolled into one glorious whole.

'Oh, Molly,' he groaned, and swept her up into his arms, whirling her round and laughing, then finally setting her down and kissing her until her socks sizzled.

'Sure?' he asked again.

She smiled. 'I'm sure. It'll be hell, but we'll survive. They're all lovely kids.'

'Seven,' he said weakly. 'Oh, my God.'

'But we've only got seven bedrooms,' Amy said.

Molly and Jack turned slowly towards the door. There, clustered in the doorway, stood Seb, defiant and victorious, with a great 'I told you so' grin on his face, and Amy and Cassie, and Tom and Philip and little Nicky.

'Molly be my mummy?' Nicky asked. Molly felt tears welling in her eyes, and hugged the little one.

'Yes, sweetheart—if that's OK with you all?'

A chorus of replies, all positive, shook the walls. Jack grinned. 'I'd better sort the attic out for Seb,' he said with a smile. 'I reckon we'll need the room.'

Seb met his eyes over the crowd, head cocked on one side. 'About this seven business,' he murmured.

'Yes?' Jack said warily.

Seb smiled smugly. 'I seem to remember a certain lecture…'

EPILOGUE

'YOU'VE got your hands full here, Jack,' Nick's father said, looking round at the children. 'Must be a sucker for punishment.'

Jack laughed. 'It's not as bad as it looks. Seb's nearly sixteen, Amy and Cassie are twelve, Tom and Philip are ten—most of them are old enough to be useful.'

'And old enough to argue,' he said with a chuckle. 'And as for Nicky and little Olivia Rose—well, I can see they'll keep you busy for a good few years yet.'

Jack looked round. Molly was pushing Nicky on the swing, while Nick's mother cuddled the baby on her lap. She was asleep, her rosebud mouth pursed, working a little from time to time. She was going to wake up soon.

'How does it feel to be honorary grandparents to three more?' he asked.

The honorary grandfather laughed. 'Just so long as you don't expect us to have them to stay all at once,' he said.

Jack chuckled. 'Would we do that to you? Besides, what would we do with ourselves with no children to look after? We'd be bored stiff.'

He glanced at Molly. The baby had started to fuss, and she scooped her up and snuggled her close. 'Are you hungry, sweetheart?' she crooned.

Jack got to his feet. 'I'll make her a cup of tea. She always gets thirsty when she feeds the baby.'

He followed her in, switched on the kettle and stood in the doorway watching her as she settled in the corner of the sofa. She patted the cushion beside her, and he lowered himself down and kissed the baby's downy head. 'Hi, precious,' he murmured. 'How's my baby girl today?'

'Greedy. I think she's going to need solids soon.'

The phone rang, and he went into the study and picked it up. 'Haddon.'

'Ah, Jack—just the man. I've had some figures on your book sales. I thought you might like to know it's just hit the bestseller list.'

His legs sagged. 'Wha—?' he groped for words, and then pulled himself together. 'Great. Thanks. Wow. Why are you in the office? It's Saturday.'

'I'm not. I'm at home. I couldn't get you yesterday, and you didn't return my call.'

He looked at the blinking light on the answer-machine. 'Sorry. We've been a bit busy.'

His editor laughed. 'Well, have a good time celebrating. I hope that wife of yours is looking after you. We're going places, Jack. Well done. Get started on the next one.'

He cradled the phone and went back in to Molly. 'That was my editor,' he said weakly. 'It's hit the bestseller list.'

Her face was a picture. 'Oh, darling, that's wonderful,' she cried, and, pulling him down beside her, she leant over and kissed him. Tears sparkled in her eyes, and he was so proud and so happy he thought he was going to burst.

'I owe it all to you,' he told her. 'Without you it wouldn't have had the warmth—and nor would I. I love you, Mrs Haddon.'

She smiled mistily. 'I love you too, Mr Haddon. You and all our lovely brood.'

'We can have a housekeeper.'

She laughed. 'I'll have help with the washing. That's my only real hate. The rest we can cope with.'

'And no more making sandwiches at stupid o'clock in the morning.'

'OK.'

'And we'll buy a car with nine seats so we can all go out together.'

'Good idea. Jack?'

He paused. 'Yes?'

'I think the kettle's boiled...'

MILLS & BOON®

Next Month's Romance Titles

♡

Each month you can choose from a wide variety of
romance novels from Mills & Boon®. Below are the new
titles to look out for next month from the Presents...™
and Enchanted™ series.

Presents...™

A BOSS IN A MILLION	Helen Brooks
HAVING LEO'S CHILD	Emma Darcy
THE BABY DEAL	Alison Kelly
THE SEDUCTION BUSINESS	Charlotte Lamb
THE WEDDING-NIGHT AFFAIR	Miranda Lee
REFORM OF THE PLAYBOY	Mary Lyons
MORE THAN A MISTRESS	Sandra Marton
THE MARRIAGE EXPERIMENT	Catherine Spencer

Enchanted™

TYCOON FOR HIRE	Lucy Gordon
MARRYING MR RIGHT	Carolyn Greene
THE WEDDING COUNTDOWN	Barbara Hannay
THE BOSS AND THE PLAIN JAYNE BRIDE	Heather MacAllister
THE RELUCTANT GROOM	Emma Richmond
READY, SET...BABY	Christie Ridgway
THE ONE-WEEK MARRIAGE	Renee Roszel
UNDERCOVER BABY	Rebecca Winters

On sale from 3rd September 1999

H1 9908

Available at most branches of WH Smith, Tesco, Asda,
Martins, Borders, Easons, Volume One/James Thin
and most good paperback bookshops